"This takes me back to a place in time when the only thing that mattered was the escape that my skateboard provided. In a place like El Paso, freedom came only to those whose trucks and wheels would hiss, bark and screech in the unforgiving dry heat. Scars and bruises worn proudly as if to say I was there."

-Cedric Bixler-Zavala, The Mars Volta

"Terry McChesney paid his dues in the rough and tumble skate town of old El Paso. Dog Tacos captures the spirit of rolling wild in the streets with a bunch of bros and powering through anything the simmering night has to offer."

-Brian Brannon, JFA

TERRY McCHESNEY

Dog Tacos

Powerslide

This book is dedicated to skateboarders everywhere.

To the young – life awaits you.
To the middle-aged – don't forget your dreams.
To the old school – keep paving paths.

Acknowledgments

I'd like to thank my wife, mentor and friend, Ruth Lozano McChesney. Her support and editing skills know no bounds. I'm grateful for Ruth's patience throughout my self-imposed exile, and her excitement and enthusiasm during the writing process. A man couldn't ask for a better editor or life partner. She is truly my inspiration and muse.

Special thanks to my good friend Brian Brannon. Brian performed most of the final edit with his laptop on the beaches of Hawaii and is responsible for the cover layout. He has a keen and experienced eye, and is an all-around excellent guy. Skateboarding and rock and roll are lucky to have him as their ambassador and I am lucky to count him as a friend.

Lastly, thanks to my brother-in-law and artist, Hector Lozano, M.D. His paintings and sculptures inspired me to return to following my dreams. I'm honored to have his artwork grace the cover of Dog Tacos.

Dog Tacos

Chapter

1

A light brown scorpion scurried across the burning sand. Its tail was arched upward as if to keep from being singed. Nearby, unknown to all living creatures, a rattlesnake slithered silently through the tall dry grass that grew around a gas meter in an alley. Its movements looked punch drunk as the morning heat took its toll. The snake was also looking for a cool place to spend the day.

It was a hot, dry May morning that would be followed by an even hotter afternoon. The day would easily reach one hundred degrees but would feel like one hundred and twenty. There hadn't been a single cloud in the sky for weeks and predictions of an impending drought had begun appearing on the news. The previous year had seen plenty of rain and everything had been green by desert standards. It had been a very rare year for El Paso.

This year, normally vibrant plants were lying brown in the scorched earth, desperately hoping the skies or some kind soul with a hose would provide the liquid nourishment they needed. The Franklin Mountains, the tail end of the majestic Rockies that forcefully divided the town, looked weak, dull and brown, providing testament to the power of the desert heat.

Mike was jolted awake as his alarm clock began its incessant call to arms. He hated the sound it made and slammed his hand down on the snooze button. It was only six-thirty but it was already over eighty degrees outside. Mike laid his head, damp with sweat, back on his pillow and drifted off to sleep. A light breeze floated through an open window and cooled him for a very welcome moment.

Ten minutes later the call to arms began again. Sitting up he felt a burning, stinging pain along the left side of his body. He stifled a scream and fell back on his bed in agony. He lay there, focusing on a poster hanging on the wall, the repetitive sounds becoming distant. The skateboarder was boardsliding a steep handrail. Mike could tell you volumes about the legendary Rob "Robocop" Kaupf. Rob was a professional skater who rode for Reptile Skateboards in San Diego. Mike had seen him skate in a demo a couple of years earlier at a local shop and had been a fan ever since.

Last night, Mike tried to 50/50 down a handrail as steep as the one in the poster. He had ollied onto it perfectly and locked his bare trucks onto the metal rail, grinding down it fast and smooth. But he wasn't prepared for the G forces that sucked him into the pavement as he landed. Instead of rolling away smoothly, his knees buckled underneath. He plowed into the cement with the entire left side of his body, head and shoulders first. Today, Mike was reaping the glory of his injuries, hefty doses of pain and humility.

He slowly pulled himself out of bed. He had an appointment at the Social Security office downtown and didn't want to be late. Mike walked into the bathroom and peeled off his t-shirt, inspecting himself in the mirror. Admiring the scratches and bruises that ran from the left side of his head to his calf, he pulled up the side of his shorts to get a better look. He hadn't cleaned up last night, so dried blood was caked everywhere, even in his hair. His shoulder, collarbone and arm felt the sorest because they had taken most of the impact. His hip had a purple-black bruise as big as a softball. Battle scars, a gory scene - one Mike was extremely proud of.

The brutality of last night's session was typical of his hard-edge skating and reflected the aggressive manner in which he exorcised his inner demons. Mike wasn't unique, most of the skaters he knew were fighting their own wars. It seemed a prerequisite for the sport.

He looked away from the mirror as his mind wandered back to his upcoming appointment. "What is it they want with me this time?" he wondered, limping to the shower. "Last time they wanted to know if I still lived with my grandmother. They could've just called. What a waste of time!"

He turned on the shower and set a timer for five minutes. As Mike stepped in, steam was already rising. The hot water shotgunned his cuts and scrapes, immediately increasing the intensity of his suffering. Cringing, he knew the stinging would subside as soon as the layers of dried blood were stripped and his cuts numbed.

As the pain disappeared, he turned up the heat and felt it melt away the stiffness in his bones. He slowly twisted from side to side, massaging his left shoulder and collarbone with the steaming spray. It felt incredibly soothing. He wished his therapy could last forever but his grandmother had a steadfast rule: "No more than five minutes." When the buzzer rang he obediently stopped the shower, just as it was helping the most.

"Gotta keep the costs down," Mike thought as he toweled off. He was more than happy to comply with his grandmother's wishes, even if it meant sacrificing his relief. He adored her and did anything she asked of him.

His parents had died in a tragic automobile accident when he was nine. He had lived with his paternal grandmother and uncle since. His grandmother had immigrated to the United States from Mexico with her family when she was an infant. Her father provided for the family modestly at best, but they never went hungry or wanted for basic necessities. She married Mike's grandfather and had two sons. Like her father, her husband was a humble provider. Before he died from an accident while working in Smelter Town, he was able to pay for the small house in which they lived. The proceeds from his nominal retirement fund and life insurance policy helped cover their daily costs.

Grandma was now an American citizen and proud of it. Her home and cooking, however, revealed her traditional Mexican roots. The outside of the house was painted bright turquoise blue and beautifully contrasted with the brown wood door and pink, yellow and light blue walls encountered inside. Her small kitchen was her command post from which she dispatched the tacos, beans and rice that she claimed no one could resist.

Mike admired himself. His brown Reptile Skateboards T-shirt and pair of baggy khaki shorts looked sharp with his RK skate shoes and hat. His cuts and bruises completed the ensemble. He'd definitely get some street cred for this. The kids at school were already impressed with his skills but after hearing of last night's 50/50 attempt, he'd be legendary.

The smell of bacon and eggs enticed Mike out of his bedroom. He took one last look in the mirror as he left. Dribbling an imaginary basketball down the hallway he slam-dunked it over his grandmother, ending with a hug.

"Morning Grandma," Mike said while sniffing the kitchen air. "That smells good."

"Good morning baby," Mike's grandmother cheerfully chirped. "What time did you say you had to be at Social Security?"

"I have an eight-thirty appointment. I wanna get there early so I don't have to wait forever like last time."

"I made fresh salsa last night. It's in the fridge."

She turned to hand Mike his breakfast and nearly dropped the plate.

"Mijo, what happened? It looks like you got run over by a car."

"It's nothing Grandma, just another fall."

"You need to see the doctor Miguel. You could have a fracture or internal injuries. Honey, you need to be more careful when you skateboard. You'll need those bones later in life, you know?"

She'd never tell Mike to stop skating. He had been such a brooding child after the accident that she didn't know how to help. She tried karate lessons when he requested them, but he still remained withdrawn. After she bought him a skateboard she began to notice an improvement in his disposition. It seemed to help him cope. She would never take it away. Besides, Mike never gave her trouble. If some cuts and bruises and the possibility of a broken bone were risks he was willing to take, then she'd let him.

She wanted Mike to have a good life, including a college education. Grandma often imagined him walking across the stage with his cap and gown and gold tassel swinging back and forth. Mike would be the first to get a degree in the family. His father had actually taken some courses at the University of Texas at El Paso but left school to fight in the Gulf War. By the time he returned he had a family to support and school was no longer an option.

Mike placed his large breakfast on the table. His grandmother always said, "It's not good to do things on an empty stomach." With his appetite, he rarely failed to clean his plate.

He grabbed his grandmother's dangerously hot salsa out of the refrigerator and spooned a large amount on his eggs. Sweat beads broke out on his forehead almost immediately after his first bite. "Peligrosa" was the only condiment the family used. Consequently, Mike spent many mornings with his head tucked under the faucet.

Mike left the house, Rob Kaupf board and backpack in tow. Near the bus stop, he spied Uncle Ralph weaving his way up the street. Tonight the cycle would begin again. At about seven, he'd leave the house to visit his "friends," stay in the bars until two in the morning when they closed and then go to some after-hours party. He rarely made it home before three. Uncle Ralph was ensnared in a vicious cycle and had been in a downward spiral for quite some time.

Ralph was a character. He fought in Operation Desert Storm and now struggled with the vivid images of the atrocities he had witnessed. As a result, he liked to hit the bottle. This sometimes led to brawls which occasionally landed him in jail. On those nights, Mike and his grandmother would have to bail him out. Uncle Ralph dealt with each aggressor differently and sometimes according to the number of drinks he had consumed and the degree of despair and pain he was experiencing. For a drunk, he was a very complex man. Despite his problems, Mike looked up to him. He was his father's older brother and the only male role model in his life.

Sometimes, a drunken Ralph let down his guard and told stories that only scratched the surface of the unspeakable realities of his war. Once, he told Mike about his best friend Charlie. They were out on patrol and Charlie stepped on a land mine. Everyone hit the ground, but Ralph was knocked off his feet. He rolled over to see what hit him and found the top half of Charlie's torso. Ralph said he'd never forget the vacant look in his friend's eyes. Then and there, he realized there is no such thing as life, just preparation for death.

On another catastrophic day, his squad went on patrol and rolled upon a massive IED. Ralph was thrown clear of the blast's effects. His fate was sealed as he witnessed the violent deaths of his mates. Those who didn't die from the explosion lost limbs or the use of them. He carried the wounded to a safe place for MediVac. When the helicopters arrived, he alone placed the mutilated corpses of his brothers in body bags. The Silver Star was bestowed upon him for his heroics, the Purple Heart for his injuries. Uncle Ralph could not escape the hellish source of his honors, maintaining he drank to forget the awful memories he brought back.

For his part in the conflict, the government now paid Ralph a monthly stipend that covered his food and rent. Every month when the check arrived, he complained, "It's not enough to wipe my ass with." What he really meant was he couldn't afford to buy cigarettes or alcohol. In order to compensate for the check's shortcomings, Ralph wrenched on his friends' cars and motorcycles. The extra work helped him support his addictions. This was Ralph's life, the life of a war veteran - a hero.

Uncle Ralph waved at Mike and shouted, "Where you going little bro?"

"Downtown. Careful Tio! You need to get to bed."

Several people were waiting at the bus stop. Mike recognized a girl he'd seen at school. He didn't know her well enough to start a conversation, so he sat down in silence.

Uncle Ralph stumbled over to the bus stop, smiling at Mike and the girl.

"Here Mikey m'boy. Twenty dollars. It was a good night at the poker table."

"Thanks, Unks but don't you need this?"

"Mikey my boy, I had a good night," Ralph said, pressing his face close to his nephew's. "A really good night! In fact, by the time I left the table, I had everyone's money and a couple of watches to boot. I even had a guy ready to put down the pink slip on his car. Hooo, boy! I was on fire last night!"

"Congratulations. Sounds like a good time."

"Yeah, I'll have to tell you about it sometime," he smiled and winked as he turned and sauntered toward the house. "Yep, it was a good night my boy," he drawled over his shoulder, "it was a damn good night."

The girl giggled at Mike. She paused for a second, then mustered, "I-I've seen you at school. You're a junior aren't you?"

"Yep. How about you?"

"I'm a freshman."

"I'm Mike. What's your name?"

"Shy."

"Shy?"

Shy giggled, looking down at her feet. "My real name is Cheyenne, but everyone calls me Shy."

Mike smiled. "You going downtown?"

"No, my grandmother's sick. I'm taking care of her until my aunt gets off work. It's easier for me to miss school than for her to miss work."

"Sorry," Mike replied. "About your grandmother, not school."

"Thanks. How 'bout you? Where are you going?"

"Downtown." Mike left it at that.

Mike's bus pulled up. Mechanically, he followed the other passengers, turning to look at Cheyenne before getting on. "See you around," he called.

Shy waved and smiled sweetly. "See you."

Mike tossed his coins into the collection slot. He walked past the front rows where all the maids from Mexico sat and headed toward the back. Housekeepers didn't get paid much in El Paso. Yet, thousands crossed the border every day, earning just enough money to scratch out a decent living back home. He looked at the women, incessantly babbling, oblivious to everything but their conversation.

"What could they be talking about?" Mike pondered. Their hand gestures and facial expressions suggested sophisticated discussions on topics like world politics and quantum physics. Mike decided these weren't matters they would entertain. Ironically, the subject under scrutiny was the governing party of Mexico that was in danger of losing its majority rule in Congress. The women were unanimous in their support of the controlling group. They commented on the oppressive and criminal nature of the opposition. "How could they return to power so soon?" "Corruption" was the general consensus.

Behind the domestic contingent were elderly men and women who no longer drove and used the bus as their primary source of transportation. Most of them went downtown to shop or walk around. They would walk slowly, taking up most of the sidewalk so it was hard to get around them. The more fragile sometimes used their canes and walkers to decelerate traffic, bringing the flow of moving bodies to a near halt and frustrating those behind them.

Mike thought of his grandmother and hoped she would never have to deal with getting old and slow. He knew her aging was inevitable but it was difficult to accept. Grandma was a vibrant woman who was never sick and religiously walked two miles a day around the neighborhood. At sixty-seven, she was aging well.

He recognized one of the older folks. The old man often stood in the plaza, preaching with a Bible in his hand. He loved to thump the Good Book and tell people what they were doing wrong under the "watchful eyes of God." Favoring the hellfire and damnation sermon to convert evil-doers, the preacher affirmed they were all destined to burn in hell for eternity unless they repented their sins. Mike thought the self-proclaimed holy man was merely crazy and liked to pass judgment on everyone. Whenever he was at the Plaza, Mike avoided walking anywhere near him.

Making his way to the back of the bus he noticed a beautiful brown-skinned, dark-eyed girl. He couldn't take his eyes off her as he passed. She was classically beautiful and dressed colorfully. He guessed she was probably a legal secretary or a cosmetic sales clerk at one of the downtown department stores. "Man, she's hot," he thought as he stretched out in a seat in the last row.

She got off a few stops later. Watching her saunter up to a nearby house, Mike realized she was just a maid. An old lady opened the door and the girl disappeared. He found it hard to believe she would be cleaning other people's toilets and floors. It seemed so wrong. "If I were rich," Mike thought, "I'd sweep her off her feet and make sure she never had to work such a lousy job again."

The reality was that he was poor. In fact, his family lived well below the poverty level. Mike had never wanted for anything, except that one Christmas when he was nine. That year, he had wanted his parents to be alive again. He painfully learned never to wish for anything out of his reach. He knew the odds were stacked against him in life, just like they were stacked against the stunning young girl.

"It's not fair," he brooded. "She's too beautiful to be a maid and I'm too smart and handsome to be poor."

He didn't understand how anyone could work at such an undignified job. The housekeepers, however, were willing to perform menial jobs because the pay was good. They would make more than those who stayed in Mexico to work in the factories. At the maquiladoras pay was less than twenty five dollars a week. A maid in El Paso could make twice that a day.

The bus lurched forward roughly, snapping Mike back to the ride. Most of the bus was empty as they were nearing San Jacinto Plaza. A few passengers had boarded while he was lost in thought. One passenger, a large, bald biker with a long, gray beard, braided and hanging to his chest, had taken a seat nearby. His muscle shirt was stretched to capacity by his ample waistline and tattoos were visible on every part of his exposed arms and legs. He even had some on his face and head. This was one of the meanest, strangest looking men Mike had ever seen. Looking closer, he spotted a Bandido's tattoo on his shoulder and determined his motorcycle must be in the shop. "Why else would a guy like that take the bus?" he mused.

Just then they pulled up to the plaza. All buses were required to do a mandatory ten minute pit stop on arrival. Five buses lined the square and dozens of people milled around outside. As Mike stepped off, he watched the old Bible-thumper walk to his pulpit and the Bandido in the direction of the shops. Mike strode away from the preacher and the biker and headed toward the Federal Building.

A mass of suits and skirts crowded the sidewalks. Workers broke off and disappeared each time they passed an office building. Nearing the Federal Building, the sidewalks had emptied, allowing Mike to skate the last few blocks. At first he was in pain from his battle wounds, but he soon felt better and was able to comfortably gyrate his board. Mike was too young to appreciate how quickly his body was healing, the privilege of youth. He only understood the glory of his board beneath his feet and the freedom that riding it generated.

Smacking his tail, he caught the front truck and entered the rotating door. The lobby was a madhouse. A crowd, five deep, blocked the directory. He waited his turn and looked for Mrs. Johnson. She was on the second floor.

He quickly ran up the stairs, springing two steps at a time out of habit. On the second floor, he turned left and found himself at the information desk. The receptionist looked up, took down Mike's information and promptly ordered him to have a seat. He was momentarily distracted by her extremely attractive bi-colored eyes and stood in place. She repeated her order, pointing toward the waiting area.

There must have been at least fifty people in the small room. Unfortunately, there were only thirty cheap plastic chairs, the kind you find in kids' cafeterias. The overflow stood on the fringes of the room, looking bored and impatient, wishing they had one of those hard, uncomfortable seats. Mike walked in and joined the forlorn crowd. Most of the people were older and Hispanic. Of course, this wasn't surprising, as most of El Paso's population was Mexican. Some of the younger women had children who were running around the room screaming and touching everything in sight. Many of the elderly patrons shot dirty looks at the women, who were oblivious to the disapproving glares and their unruly offspring.

Occasionally, a mother would call her children and scold them for their behavior, only to let them return to their mischief unsupervised. At one point, a boy who looked about five years old ran into a dispenser. Pamphlets rained all over the child, who sat there bewildered and crying. A few of the patrons, including Mike, came to the child's rescue, helping pick up the mess. The extent of the mother's role was to tell her child to sit still and be quiet.

Mike swore he'd never have a wife or kids who behaved like that.

Chapter
2

After an hour, a stocky, intimidating clerk called his name. Brick House played in his head while he walked behind her. The melody brought a smile to his face as she motioned him toward an open door.

Mrs. Johnson was on the phone and signaled Mike to sit. She was beautiful and appeared to be in her early thirties. Her cashmere sweater firmly gripped her hourglass body. Her face was bright, smiling and flawless. He silently mouthed a thank you. Mrs. Johnson pursed her lips together sensuously and put one finger in the air to indicate she'd be a minute.

"Take your time," Mike said to himself, spellbound by her beauty. She slowly swiveled her seat until it faced the window, continuing her conversation with her back to him.

"Damn," he thought dejectedly.

The office was filled with interesting things. He studied the framed documents on the walls, some from colleges she had attended, others for excelling in her profession. A few were awards from marathons and mountain bike races she had entered. There was even a framed magazine article naming her the female U.S. mountain biker most likely to compete in the next Olympics. Mike was impressed.

Knick-knacks lined the edge of her desk. She had placed them there for the entertainment of her younger clients. Mike was fascinated by the little black and white penguins that would rock back and forth but couldn't be knocked down, like those Weebles that wobbled. He amused himself while Mrs. Johnson continued her conversation.

A short time later she hung up, turned around and tidied her desk. She took some long sips from her coffee mug, put on her reading glasses, and finally made eye contact. Mike thought he'd pass out.

"Hi Mike," she said warmly. "I'm Mrs. Johnson, your case worker." She shuffled some papers. "I believe someone here saw you this time last year. Is that right?"

"Yep. Mrs. Metcalf."

Mrs. Johnson looked up and studied his short response. His nervousness was evident, as she asked him to stand and turn. Policy required the Agency regularly check on the welfare of those under its care. "We want to make sure you're in good shape. You seem to be doing very well," Mrs. Johnson determined by Mike's size and clean clothes. "Is there anything you'd like to talk to me about Mike?" She moved her reading glasses down and looked over them.

"No, ma'am," Mike politely responded.

"I see. Does your grandmother give you any money? You know an allowance of some sort."

"Fifteen dollars a week."

"What do you spend the money on?"

"Skateboards mostly."

"That's a nice one you got there."

"Thanks." Mike beamed.

She tapped her finger on her lips and smiled. Mike was mesmerized.

"How'd you get those bruises?"

Mike swelled with pride but tried to sound casual. "On my skateboard. I was doing a 50/50 down a handrail." Mike used his hand to show her the move he was describing.

"Oh I've seen pictures of that. It must be hard."

"Yeah it is. I'm sure you get bruised too."

"What?"

"You know. You mountain bike, don't you?"

"Oh. Yes. Do you?"

"No. I saw your article over there," Mike nodded in the direction of the frame.

Mrs. Johnson laughed. She pulled up her pant leg and showed Mike a small trail of scabs that climbed up her calf. "Got this when I stepped down onto my chain rings. Skateboarding on handrails. You must be good, or crazy."

"Probably a little of both. I'd love to be a pro someday. That or prosecute drunk drivers."

Mrs. Johnson's smile lessened and she quietly said, "I want to talk to you just a little more, if you don't mind."

"I don't mind," Mike responded.

"What do you mean 'prosecute drunk drivers'?" she queried.

"My parents were killed by a drunk driver," he replied, his mood darkening. "Everyone deserves justice."

"Do you want to talk about it?"

"Not really." Mike hung his head.

"Have you been evaluated by any of our counselors?"

"I used to see Beverly Diaz."

"I'd like for you to meet with her again. What do you think?"

"Just once?" Mike worried about spending his summer in counseling.

"Let's have an initial meeting and we'll see. Beverly will contact you. It was good seeing you. Maybe we'll meet again soon. You know, your benefits expire when you turn twenty-one."

"Yes ma'am. They tell me that every time."

"That's good to know. We'll be in touch, then. Good luck with school and take care."

She smiled again and showed him the door. He started down the stairway, running into Beverly Diaz at the bottom. Beverly had been Mike's counselor when his parents first passed away.

"Hi Mike," Beverly chirped. "Fancy seeing you here. How's everything at Casa Grandma?" She always called his house Casa Grandma. It cracked him up.

Beverly was a petite brunette who always wore a pixie hair cut. Although it had been several years since they had first met, she was still beautiful.

"Hola Señora Díaz," Mike replied. "Casa Grandma esta excelente." He always answered that question in Spanish, probably because it seemed to please Beverly so much.

"What happened? You look horrendous!" She was shocked by his injuries.

"Just skating. No big deal." He tried to impress her with his bravado.

"What are you doing here?" she asked. "Seeing another counselor behind my back?"

Mike turned red. "No, I saw my case worker. She's checking on me." He rolled his eyes as he spoke. "She says I should see you."

"OK, Mike. I'm running late but we'll make an appointment soon."

"See you Beverly." Mike waved at her as she started up the stairs. He was glad to see her again. She reminded him of his mother, smart, pretty and funny. In fact, after the accident, she would take him along with her children to the zoo or amusement park.

He exited through the main door and was blanketed by the heat of the day. It was ten fifteen and over ninety degrees. Mike needed to catch the bus. Figuring there was no way he'd make it to school before lunch, he decided to skate reconnaissance to the plaza.

The sidewalks were vacant, allowing him to skate in solitude. A quick, refreshing breeze ruffled his hair. Approaching a banked wall, he crouched and popped a wallie off of it. The takeoff was perfect but the landing sketchy. His wheels bit into his board and he toppled forward. He fell with a thud, cuts and bruises screaming at him.

"Damn injuries," Mike muttered.

At that very moment he noticed a perfect parking block. He pushed quickly and ollied onto it in a 5-0 grind. His rear truck made a noise like a knife being sharpened. At the end of the parking block, he spun off fakie. The board was pointed slightly too high and the tail spiked into the asphalt. Mike plowed backwards into the ground. He hit his uninjured side and rolled with the fall.

Gingerly brushing off tiny rocks and pieces of glass embedded in his forearm, he smeared small droplets of blood in the process. His limp was barely noticeable as he hiked onward.

The bus was nearly empty when he boarded. Other than an old couple sitting up front who had been shopping, Mike was the only passenger. As they rolled forward, he walked down the aisle, past the empty seats, once again grabbing a seat in the last row.

Mike heard his school's lunch buzzer sound as he stepped onto the sidewalk. The first person he saw was Angela, his best friend David's younger sister. She waved and ran up to him with a big, beaming smile. Her long brown hair and breasts bounced with every stride she took. Mike found the whole thing erotic and had to shake himself out of it before she reached him.

"Hey Mike. Where've you been?" Angela asked casually. "I wanted ... What happened? You look terrible!"

"Oh this, it's nothing. Just a little spill." Mike's pride showed as he spoke. "Where's D?"

"David? Why look for him? I'm right here." she pouted and looked at him with mock indignation. He melted but said nothing. Her advances were becoming increasingly difficult to sidestep.

"So, you know where he is?" Mike pressed.

"Well if you want to be that way about it, he's hanging out with the Hessians at the picnic tables. You could always have lunch with me."

"But David's your brother, you know?"

"You can still be friends with David and have lunch with me. I didn't ask you to marry me." Tears welled in her eyes. Mike was perplexed. His allegiance was at odds.

"Sorry. I need to talk to him about tonight."

"Sure Mike. You better find your sidekick before lunch ends," Angela retorted as she turned and stormed off. Mike was dumbstruck.

At the picnic tables, Mike found David trying tricks with about ten other skaters. They resembled the windup toys he often saw in store windows downtown. He especially loved the wind up monkey that banged little cymbals. One skater lost his balance. His board shot away before he snorkeled through some asphalt. Most laughed at his misfortune, David offered a hand and asked if he was OK. Then he picked his board up, spotted his friend and walked over.

"Hey, where've you been dude?" David asked. "I didn't see you this morning."

"Downtown."

"You still have to do that?"

"Yep. Gotta keep my benefits."

"Benefits? Like what, free tickets to concerts or something? Hook us up with tickets to The Mars Volta concert!"

"Did you get dropped on your head, dude? Seriously!"

"Take it easy Miguel. I'm just giving you a hard time." David jabbed Mike's shoulder and laughed playfully. "You seem a little stressed vato! Take a chill pill. Doctor's orders."

Mike cocked his eyebrow and glared at David. He wondered if lunch with Angela might have been a better idea.

They tucked their boards under the table and David sat down. He opened a brown paper sack and pulled out two subs, a medium sized bag of salt and vinegar chips, and two dollars. Without a word, he slid Mike the money who snatched the cash and ran into the machine shop, appearing moments later with two sodas. David kept one sandwich and rolled the other toward Mike's spot. Mike tossed David a soda and sat down. Their movements were synchronized, as if they'd done this many times before.

"Thanks," Mike said. "Your mom's the best. I was worried you'd eat my food."

"Yeah, right. You know my mom would kill me. I'll never forget the time she sent me to school with lunch for you and nothing for me because I ate your cookie the day before. I'm lucky you gave me half your lunch. She thinks you're the shiz!"

Since grade school, Mrs. Davis had been preparing Mike's lunches. His favorite was the roast beef sandwich au jus with horseradish sauce. David and Angela also loved it. Consequently, it was a regular lunchtime meal. Mike especially liked Mrs. Davis' intolerably and irresistibly hot horseradish sauce. He claimed it could peel the paint off a barn. Tears poured every time he ate the overpowering condiment. She had purchased a rare variety of horseradish root in a remote fishing village in

Scandinavia and had managed to successfully cultivate it in her El Paso garden. It was her pride and joy.

The end-of-lunch bell rang as the boys took their last bites. They grabbed their books and boards, and hurried to the building. Inside, the halls were alive with a flurry of students racing to their lockers. The boys weaved and battled through the throngs on their way to geometry. Entering the room, they nodded to a couple of friends and sat in their desks toward the back.

"Yo D, we gonna tear up that Forbidden Zone tonight?" Mike questioned in his best gangster voice.

David laughed and rolled his eyes. "Word bro! I've been waiting all week. Da Forbidden Zone. I can't wait till summer comes and we can skate all day. Only two more weeks dude!" David held his hand up and Mike high-fived him. The conversation followed Mike the rest of the day. School couldn't end fast enough.

After school, he hurried home to change his clothes and eat, his thoughts consumed with the evening's plans. He was picking up David, then Cedric and Jimmy at seven. Downtown was a skater's paradise at night. Not only did the area become a skatepark for the boys, it was a great place to people watch and see unusual and interesting things, like hookers and drunks.

Mike was several blocks from his house when he heard his name called. He spun and saw Angela with her best friends Patti and Christie. Angela hugged her friends goodbye and ran to Mike.

He couldn't help but notice her recently

acquired curves and the heavier makeup. He momentarily forgot she was David's little sister. She was a stunning girl.

"Hi, Mike! Whatcha doing?" Angela asked, a little out of breath. She was in a better mood this time.

"Home to eat, then skate with your brother."

Angela made a face and snapped, "David, again? When are we gonna hang out?"

Mike blushed at her forwardness. Beneath his crumbling façade, he tested the waters.

"I'm going to Chico's, wanna go?" Mike asked, surprised by his sudden boldness.

"Is this a date?" Angela blurted, caught off guard by Mike's unexpected invitation.

Mike's ears were burning. He wanted to shout, "Yes!" Instead, he said, "Just tacos."

She searched Mike's eyes and only saw the shield he and all men use when their feelings bubble too close to the surface. She pursed her lips indignantly and turned toward her house. Without looking back, she stated, "I'll be ready in fifteen minutes."

"OK. Fifteen minutes." Mike said feebly. He walked up the sidewalk to his front door, watching Angela walk away, hips swaying back and forth.

Chapter
3

Angela was on the porch swing when Mike arrived. Her hair was tied up in a ponytail, her tank top and tight jeans highlighting her assets, her face radiating. Mike determined her resemblance to Kat Dennings in *Nick and Norah's Infinite Playlist* was unmistakable.

"David wouldn't mind if I went out with Angela. It shouldn't cut into our skate time too much. I could do both. I could skate with David during the day and go out with Angela at night. Shut up! I'm here!" Mike's thoughts invaded his reality.

Angela sidled up to Mike and gave him a big hug. Mike reciprocated, straight and stiff like a board, worried Mrs. Davis or David might see. Sensing his reluctance, Angela released her bear hug. She briefly stared at him, grabbed his hand and proceeded to lead him toward Chico's.

"Let's go to your favorite restaurant," she giggled. "I can't wait to eat some soggy rolled tacos."

"My tacos never get soggy," he replied. "I order them with the sauce on the side. They stay crunchy longer that way. I hate soggy tacos."

"Wow. That's deep. Sounds like you've thought about it. Kinda scary really. Remember the time we had stew for supper and you wouldn't eat the carrots or celery? You're picky."

Mike laughed in acknowledgement. It was a source of frustration for his family. Whenever he went to a restaurant, he rarely ordered exactly from the menu. He had been ordering his tacos dry as long as he could remember.

Chico's average customers were trying to stretch their dollars, mostly low-income families and high school kids on dates. They had a cult-like following in El Paso and were often filled to capacity. There was already a sizable crowd when they arrived. Mike showed Angela to the only open table. "What do you want?" he asked.

"I'll have an order of tacos and a small root beer," she replied. "Not much ice, please."

"Who's being picky now?"

Angela smiled. "You're such a tease Mikey."

Mike remembered his mother calling him that when he was little. It was comforting to hear it again. He was hungry and had a long night ahead. At the counter, he asked for a hot dog, an order of tacos with the sauce on the side, an order of fries and a large root beer, then placed his date's order. He knew every item on the menu and loved them all. He usually got extra cheese but didn't want to look like a pig.

Mike and Angela were acquainted with the family at the next table and socialized with them until their number was called. He went to the counter and picked up the tray with her food first. He brought it to the table before going back for his.

"Thanks, Mikey. You're such a gentleman," Angela remarked when he got back. "Your Grandmother really taught you well."

"What do you mean?"

"Well, let's see. You held the door, ordered, and brought my food to the table first. That's the mark of a true gentleman."

"Just good manners." He was embarrassed as much from the narration as he was from being called a gentleman. Hanging out with Angela was going to take some serious adjusting.

"See. That's what I mean! You don't even know how special you are. I wish more boys were like you. Most of the guys at school are geeks or jerks."

"Great, now I'm always gonna wonder geek or jerk." Mike chuckled as Angela laughed.

She spied Mike's full tray of food and exclaimed, "You sure eat a lot! What's that?"

"Hotdog."

"It looks like a chili burger. Is it good?"

Chico's hot dogs were almost as legendary as their tacos. They started with two bright red, grilled hotdogs split lengthwise. They were then topped with chili beans, mustard and pickles on a charred hamburger bun. With good reason, these were Mike's favorite. For Mike's sixth birthday, his parents surprised him with a small party "catered" by Chico's. As he often did when trying new food, Mike took a bite of his father's hot dog. To the six-year-old boy it was a rite of passage into manhood. He was hooked from that day on. Since his small stomach wouldn't allow him to consume a full hot dog and order of tacos, his mother would invariably pack the leftover sandwich for lunch the next day. Nowadays, the leftover school lunch was a distant memory but he never failed to order or completely devour the strange looking dog whenever he had the chance.

"Want some?" Mike started to tear a piece off for Angela.

"How about letting me just have a bite?" Angela asked.

Mike wasn't used to sharing his food. In fact, he never let anyone eat directly from his plate. He was a little phobic about germs and he hesitated a moment.

"Well?" Angela asked. "Can I have some?"

"Uh sure," Mike said. "I spaced for a second. Here you go."

Mike handed the hot dog to Angela, but she wrapped her small hand over his and leaned over. He became flushed but held on tight, watching as she took a small, dainty bite. After she finished her demure but controlling nibble, she released her grip and reached for her napkin.

Mike could barely see where the hot dog was bitten. He looked up at Angela who was still chewing. When she finished, she dabbed her mouth with her napkin over and over as if she had made a mess. The size of her bite, the endless chewing, and the overuse of her napkin was comical. He was smitten.

"Have you ever eaten a hot dog here before?" he asked.

"Not before today. You may have to order me one of those next time."

"Yeah," Mike smiled. "Chico's makes the best hot dogs. They're even better than the ones I ate in

Chicago."

Angela nodded and smiled coyly at Mike. She had never seen him passionate about anything but school and skateboarding. It seemed strange to her he was so enthusiastic about a hot dog on a hamburger bun. She found Mike's intensity very appealing.

Angela could watch Mike skateboard all day. It was intense like ballet. She never understood how, through all his spinning and jumping, he kept his board attached to his feet. He looked so graceful, yet powerful when he skated. He even looked good falling.

As Mike took a bite from his hot dog, Angela noticed he had mustard on the corner of his mouth. She reached out gently and wiped it away with a napkin, trailing one of her long fingernails against his cheek. Mike immediately got goose bumps and summoned his will power and exercise of restraint. Instead of doing something he might regret, he picked up his hot dog and took a rather large mouthful.

"Careful Mikey," Angela teased, "You could choke on that. I don't think I could give you the Heimlich maneuver."

Mike blushed and finished chewing. He realized how silly it must look to her. After all, she took such small bites. Mike, on the other hand, was used to eating with his friends, and their preferred method of consumption was to eat big and fast. They both giggled. Angela's eyes toyed with Mike's. Mike's slowly revealed weaknesses in his armor.

He was enjoying his time alone with Angela but was eager to meet up with David. Mike policed the table and threw the trash away. Angela was waiting by the door when he returned. He held the door for her and they slowly walked home.

David and Angela were "military brats" when the Army transferred Mr. Davis to Fort Bliss. The family had previously lived in many cities throughout the world and had settled in El Paso. The kids were grateful to finally stay in one place. Mike had just moved in with his grandmother and was riding his bicycle when he saw them in their front yard. He offered to show them the nearby park with the big swing set. From that day on Mike and David were inseparable.

Tonight, Mike was seeing Angela in a different light. She was no longer "David's little sister". He was already thinking about their next date. Mike was conflicted. He wanted to stay with Angela but was anxious to skate with his friends. Until now, schooling and his grandmother had been the only things more important than skateboarding.

Big Larry, the local skateboard shop owner once said, "I lose most of my customers when they become interested in cars or girls." Mike had no intention of becoming a statistic and vowed to skateboard until he died. So far, at seventeen and with four years under his belt, Mike was holding true. He was unaware he had already moved Angela to the top of his list.

"I've gotta meet David. What are you doing tonight?" Mike asked.

"I'm seeing a movie with Christie and her sister Lauren, but we haven't decided which one. There isn't a whole lot showing right now." Angela wrinkled her nose.

"So why go? Why don't you do something else?"

Angela laughed indignantly. "A certain someone hasn't asked me out yet. If he did," she added dramatically, "I'd probably say yes."

"I'll have to save you from your anguish some day," he grinned.

Angela smiled and kissed him gently on the cheek. "Thanks for taking me to Chico's. I had a really good time. Maybe we can do it again soon."

"I'll check my calendar," Mike teased. "I had a good time too."

"We don't have to see a movie. I'll be happy sitting with you on the porch, talking. It doesn't have to be a date."

Mike and Angela spoke very little the remainder of the way. David was on the porch when they returned. He had a wheel off of his board and was cleaning its bearings. Angela said good bye to Mike, hugged him and went inside.

Mike looked at David. He knew it was coming. He could feel it. Suddenly, David laughed.

"I always knew you'd go out with Angela."

"What do you mean, you always knew?" Mike asked, his face turning red. "I didn't even know."

David enjoyed making his friend uneasy. "Remember when Angela was in first grade? She was being picked on by that group of girls. You waited after school and stood up for her. You even stood up to one of their big brothers. That night, Mom said you were Angela's knight in shining armor. I always thought you guys would go out."

"Man. You already have us married. Anything else I should know?"

"Yeah, Angela turns into a werewolf when there's a full moon." David laughed and grabbed Mike around the back of his neck. "No matter what, you're always my main man. We have too much history. Anyway, you'd be much better for her than most of the guys I know."

"Good, I want to ask Angela out."

"Angie, jo Angie! Come here." David shouted sounding like Scarface. "Mikey's got a little something he'd like to ask jou."

Angie came back outside. She looked at Mike and blushed. She turned to David. "Yes?"

"Mike wants to ask you something. Don't you Mike?"

Mike avoided direct eye contact with either of them. His neck and ears instantly turned hot, to the point of burning. Finally, he looked up with his best James Dean pose and stammered, "Would you like to go out? Maybe a movie and dinner? You know a real date."

"You mean it?" Angela was looking at David.

"Yeah, I think he does." David laughed, shrugging his shoulders.

"How about six tomorrow?" Mike stammered, surprised and relieved by David's support.

"OK, six it is. I'll be ready and waiting. What movie?"

"I don't know. You pick."

"OK. I'll choose a good one."

"Have fun with Christie and Lauren," Mike teased as she turned to leave.

Angela looked over her shoulder, flirtingly wagged a finger, and stopped mid-stride. She turned back toward Mike, edged up to him, threw her arms around his neck and planted a big kiss on his cheek, exhaling as she pulled away. Her warm breath sent chills through his body. He was unprepared for her display of emotions and turned a deeper shade of red. He seriously considered staying home. Angela's spell had been cast. Chuckling to himself, he vowed once again, nothing would get in the way of his skateboarding with David. It was more of a plea than a promise. The temptation of Angela would be exceedingly difficult to overcome.

Angela skipped away and quickly disappeared inside.

David smirked at Mike and punched him hard on his injury-free shoulder. "Letting my little sister kiss you! You should be ashamed of yourself."

"If you had said that ten minutes ago, I might've believed you."

Mike rubbed his sore shoulder and kicked at David's back end. David spun around and missed catching Mike's leg. Mike squatted and swept David's feet out from under him.

"Damn karate lessons," David groaned, lying on his back.

"Sorry. I get carried away." Mike couldn't help but laugh as he picked David up.

Mike's sweep hurt David more than he was willing to show. They had taken karate lessons together, but David wasn't as good as Mike who had accumulated several trophies. When the boys decided to stop taking lessons, their instructor begged Mike to continue. He even spoke with his grandmother. The instructor's disregard of David still hurt.

Karate had done much to prepare them for their next sport. The rigorous exercise regimens they followed had resulted in strong, rippled abdomens. The combat training they practiced taught them to absorb impacts and fall correctly. When skating, falling was a given, and knowing how to fall was a valuable skill.

The boys walked to Mike's to get his board and shoes. His grandmother and uncle were in the kitchen eating a late supper. Uncle Ralph was usually with his "friends" by this time on a Friday evening. Mike found it strange to find him at home.

"Hi, boys. Would you like something to eat?" called out Grandma. "There's left over pot roast and potatoes."

"No thanks Grams." Mike replied. "We've already eaten."

"Your Grandma's a great cook. I'm stuffed." Uncle Ralph leaned back and patted his stomach. "So what you two got planned? It's a perfect night to be out."

"We're gonna skate with Jimmy and Cedric. We should be home by midnight." Mike kept it brief and started moving toward the front door. He didn't want his grandmother to find out about the Forbidden Zone or the party.

"OK Mikey. You boys be careful," his grandmother tugged his shirt as he passed. "Stay out of trouble and be home by midnight." She always told him to be careful when he went out. It was her code for "good bye" and "I love you".

"We will. See you later." Mike bent down and kissed her on the forehead. Uncle Ralph raised his hand and Mike slapped him a high five as he passed by.

Getting on their boards, David took the lead. They were meeting Jimmy and Cedric on Montana Street to catch the bus downtown.

Spotting Cedric waiting alone at the bus stop, David crossed Montana and asked, "Hey Ced, where's Jimmy?"

"Sick. He's gotta stay home," Cedric replied.

"What's wrong? Is he going to be all right?" Mike queried further.

"Don't know. Food poisoning I think. He went to a doctor but he's feeling pretty bad."

Cedric went to school with Mike and David, Austin High School, home of the Panthers. Jimmy went to their rival school, El Paso High, home of the Tigers. Each year the schools' football teams played a game for "The Claw," a coveted trophy with a big cat's paw. "The Claw" could pass for a panther's paw, as well as a tiger's. The boys didn't let school rivalries affect their relationship. They were friends and skaters first, students second.

"Too bad," David exclaimed. "He's cool."

"Yeah," Cedric agreed, "Hey, you guys wanna head across the border for some Dog Tacos after we skate?"

"I don't think so," Mike said adamantly, scrunching his nose and flaring his nostrils. "I'll stick with Chico's."

Cedric laughed, enjoying Mike's reaction. "Dude, they have the best tacos. You won't believe how good they are."

"Sounds good," David interjected. "We can go there before the party. It's Friday night, discos and beautiful girls! C'mon, Mike!"

Mike shrugged, hesitant to leave the safety of the United States. He remembered crossing the bridge with his father to fill the car with cheap lead-filled gas. It was a dirty border town, separated from El Paso by the sometimes barely flowing Rio Grande. His dad called the cities the "Twin Sisters" because they shared so much. He said millions of people lived in Juarez when the weather warmed and the work in America was plentiful. Migrants came from all over Mexico and Central America, stopping at the border towns before hiring a coyote to help them illegally cross. They'd swim or float on inner tubes in the dark of night. Some would hide underneath the smuggler's car seat, crammed into a suffocating, uncomfortable space not meant for any living being, all for a chance at the American dream, or at least a decent-paying job. The U.S. Border Patrol, "La Migra," would spend their days and nights rounding up as many illegals as they could find. His dad had said their plight reminded him of salmon swimming upstream while the bears plucked them out of the water.

Juarez was also a tourist town. On weekends, teenagers and American soldiers flocked to the city's bars, where drinks were cheap and readily sold to the under-aged. Discothèques, bars, and hawkers lined the main street, tempting young partygoers and soldiers eager to spend their small paychecks. Most would make it back without incident, but the unfortunate few would spend the night in a cramped, urine-soaked cell until the acceptable bribe had been paid to the proper authorities.

"That's our ride," Cedric pointed at the approaching city bus. The boys climbed on board, ready for a night of adventure. They took their customary seats at the rear. Several people looked curiously at their boards. The painted grip tape and strange graphics always drew attention.

The maids and old people were replaced by tweenagers, mostly male, dressed up and smelling of cheap cologne. A group of beautiful girls sat in the front seats appearing self-conscious as they huddled tightly together. Another group cuddled with their boyfriends.

Holding his nose and gasping for air, Cedric whispered, "Who's wearing the cologne?"

Mike and David burst out laughing as just about every male on the bus was wearing a strong dose of toilet water. They sat for most of the ride in silence observing the passengers. At some point, each skater fell in love with one of the beautiful girls. A girl with bleached-blonde hair several rows ahead caught Mike's attention. She was twisting her hair as she chatted with her friends. He could only see her hair, shoulders and part of her face. She was gorgeous.

As the bus neared the edge of downtown, the blonde pushed the buzzer. She and her friends stood up to exit. Mike couldn't wait to get a good look at her. As they departed, the blonde told her girlfriends, "You'll absolutely love dancing at the Old Plantation. It's the best gay bar in town. They make their drinks strong, like their men." The blonde put his hand to his face and giggled. "You know how I love strong men," he sang at them. More giggling. Mike was shocked and embarrassed as he realized his mistake. He turned to look at his friends, hoping they hadn't noticed his intent gazes. They were focused on other girls, completely oblivious to Mike's fascination with the faux-female and subsequent discomfort.

The bus pulled up to the plaza and opened its doors. The driver gathered his seat cushion and lunch box and stepped outside to enjoy his break. Several drivers were already assembled and he joined them with a few handshakes and back slaps before sitting down to his meal. The friends stepped into the night, ready to thrash and have fun on the city streets. They had no clue this night would change their lives forever.

Chapter
4

Several buses were parked in cue on Mills Street. As each driver's break ended, another bus would close its doors and thread its way back through the city, collecting and depositing the humans. The plaza was completely transformed. During the day, the constant stream of people made it almost impossible to skate from one side to the other. The throngs of daytime workers and shoppers had disappeared, replaced by suspicious groups gathered in dark clusters at the unlit benches.

Mike and David hadn't skated downtown with Cedric and were anxious to show him their favorite spots. Likewise, Cedric couldn't wait to show his friends Dog Tacos, his all-time favorite taco stand. They decided to skate until nine, then walk across the border for dinner. If all went well, they'd be on their way to the party by ten.

Clack-clack, clack-clack, clack-clack. Three sets of skateboard wheels set off across the plaza. The skaters wove gracefully in and out among the benches lining the sidewalk. As they rode past the dark clusters, the smell of alcohol, tobacco and pungent marijuana smoke attacked their senses. The clusters huddled together, speaking in muffled, short sentences. They were oblivious to the skaters as they rolled past. Mike was grateful for the anonymity.

In the daytime, you could be ticketed by one of the many police officers who patrolled on foot. At night, you had to worry more about the groups huddled together in the dark. There had been stories of muggings, rapes and murders at night in the plaza. Mike's grandmother warned him to stay out of the area after nightfall. He never told her he skated in the Forbidden Zone because he didn't want to upset her.

Cedric was the first to pop an ollie, over a discarded McDonald's bag. Seeing Cedric jump set Mike's mind into gear. He neared a bench, rolled up parallel to it, popped an ollie and twisted sideways landing in a boardslide. "Schhhhhhschht…" His board sounded beautiful as it slid along the top of the bench. At the end, Mike let his momentum carry him off and back safely to the sidewalk. The trick felt smooth as he absorbed the landing with bent knees. His cuts and bruises from the night before were forgotten for the moment. Of course, a wipe out would result in the pain increasing threefold. He knew this all too well from experience and could only hope to avoid re-injury.

As they skated down the street, they worked on different moves. Most of them started with an ollie. They would slam their tail on the ground and jump up with the board as it rose. If they did it correctly, they'd land and roll away. Sometimes they'd land on a rail or curb, grinding or sliding on it. Other times they'd flip the board in a kickflip or heelflip before catching it with their feet and riding off. Their most challenging and impressive moves required a kickflip into a boardslide or grind.

David found a tall sidewalk and ollied off of it. He hovered about three feet above the street at the highest point of the jump. His wheels made a loud noise as they contacted the pavement. Mike loved the powerfully sharp, cracking sound, almost like gunfire.

They skated west toward the Abraham Chavez Theater, home of the "Rails of Death". Along the way, the streets were dark and mostly vacant, like a ghost town spread out before them. Only this one beckoned their steeds to ride over the curbs, ledges and banks. Mike gyrated back and forth as he rolled down the abandoned street, a slalom skier on pavement. It was old school.

Suddenly, he heard a noise from above. He quickly glanced up to find an older lady hanging laundry on her balcony, two stories up. She was methodical, pinning garments to the clothesline and tugging on the line twice to move it out into the breeze. She did it for each item in her basket, hanging sheets on the first line, shirts, blouses, skirts and pants on the second, and undergarments on the third. Mike was impressed with her precision. It reminded him of his grandmother.

As he observed the laundry ritual, he studied the underground civilization living above. Inhabitants were on the balconies of their small, dingy apartments, enjoying an otherwise hot El Paso evening. Some sat behind awnings as if still waiting for the sun to set behind the Franklin Mountains. Others escaped their tiny slum-like residences, treasuring the open space their small crowded porches provided. The more inspired improved their terraces with large plants, grills, tables and chairs. In reality, the plants brought gnats, the grills added to the heat, and the tables and chairs took up valuable space.

They reminded Mike of the Anasazi Indians he had read about in school, each family in their own little cave, living disregarded lives on the edge of the cliff. As Mike passed beneath, the smell of burning charcoal and searing meat stimulated his senses. His stomach reminded him they'd soon be at Dog Tacos. He wondered what Cedric found so appealing and special about this little taco stand across the border.

David was in the lead and waited at the stop light for the others before crossing to the Abraham Chavez Theater. The main entrance was guarded by a homeless man, curled up and snoring. He didn't seem to hear the loud, noisy skateboarders as they ollied, kickflipped and boardslid to their hearts' content. The boys understood his deep slumber when they spotted an empty bottle of Night Train wine by his head. As Mike contemplated his next trick, he heard a loud thud.

Cedric had landed badly and fell backwards. His board shot out from under his feet like a rocket launching horizontally. It blasted straight toward the sleeping man's head. The boys stood frozen and open-mouthed as they watched the projectile zero in. At the last moment, it hit a small rock and veered left, barely missing the drunk's head. The board made a sharp, loud, smacking sound as it hit the wall right behind him.

He awakened this time. Jumping up he shouted obscenities at the intruders. He should have appeared harmless at about five feet four inches and not much more than one hundred pounds. However, the boys were familiar with the stories of drunks doing pretty awful things downtown and didn't stick around. They grabbed their boards and propelled toward a different area of the theater at full speed.

They came upon the "Rails of Death," long, steep handrails beside the 28 stairs that led to the underground parking. They were so steep that no one had been known to ollie onto them and boardslide. Mike and David, however, had done cheater slides on them and couldn't wait to amaze Cedric with their insane skills.

Cedric took a look at the stairs and wondered aloud, "What are you guys doing? These handrails are impossible."

"We've skated them before," David commented with a big grin on his face. "They're fun. Wanna give 'em a try?"

Cedric looked more than a little apprehensive. The rails were much longer than anything he'd tried. He was sure he'd be seriously injured. He looked to Mike seeking confirmation of the mad joke they were certainly pulling on him. Instead, Mike smiled.

"I don't get it," Cedric said.

David laughed at Cedric's dismay. He was always competing with someone. Usually it was Mike, and he always lost. Tonight, David was focused on Cedric. He swaggered up to the handrails and started to climb onto them. Cedric's mouth dropped open.

Standing on top, David positioned his board, placing one hand in front to act as a brake. He put his other hand in front and stepped onto the board. David was now crouched and ready to slide.

"You guys ready?" David asked trying to milk the moment.

"Go for it!" Mike chanted. Cedric wasn't speaking. He was bewildered, and a little pale. David released his grip and slid toward the bottom. By the time he reached the mid point, his speed was uncontrollable. At the bottom, skater and board slid off. David tried to maintain control, but wasn't able to get his board completely under him on the landing. Instead, his weight, doubled by the speed, slammed him into the cement.

Cedric was visibly shaken. Mike called down, "You all right D?"

David sprung up and smiled. "That was totally awesome dudes," he said in his best Spiccoli voice. "Like uh, who's next?"

Before David had finished asking the question, Mike had already placed his board on the rail. He was excited, especially in front of his audience. Although he had successfully accomplished it many times before, the danger and risk involved gave him momentary pause. He wondered if he would ever be able to ollie on before sliding at what he believed to be an unimaginable speed. Fantasizing about bringing Rob Kaupf to slide the "Rails of Death," he convinced himself Rob could probably do it.

Squatting, Mike centered himself on his board and looked down the rail. He envisioned himself sliding down fast, landing and riding away smoothly. Soon, he regained his courage and caught his breath. He tried to keep thoughts of slamming or wrecking at bay lest they prophesize the outcome. Although he had never been hurt on the "Rails," Mike was keenly aware of the intense risks involved, and always gave them the respect they deserved.

David remained at the bottom of the stairs and called up, "I'll stay down here. I'll get a better view."

"OK. Stay out of my way! Here I come!"

Mike let go and jetted down fast, trying to dominate the effects of gravity. Despite his incredible speed, he remained relaxed, appearing almost casual. Reaching the bottom, he smoothly popped off and landed cleanly, crouching low in order to absorb the impact. He continued to speed away from the rail, turned his board sideways and screeched to a sliding stop.

"Yeah buddy!!!" David yelled, jumping up and pumping his fist into the air. "That was awesome, dude! You own it!"

Cedric slid his hands across the rails, skipping several stairs at a time as he sped to join his friends. "I thought you were joking! That was intense!"

Mike beamed as his friends voiced their accolades and patted his back. "I thought I was going to lose it! That's the fastest I've ever slid! It felt like someone had waxed the rail!"

"Too cool. You know, this was the first rail I ever slid," David said proudly. "Mike talked me into it."

"I thought you'd never do it," Mike laughed. "I was ready to go home when you finally got the nerve."

"What made you finally do it?" Cedric turned to David.

"Mike convinced me it was easier than it looked," replied David as he glared at Mike proudly.

"Was it?" Cedric genuinely wanted to know.

"I've only made it three times. I've biffed about a hundred times, so I'd say the answer is NO." David rolled his eyes.

"Then, I'm not trying it," Cedric laughed. "Maybe next time." Cedric was relieved at David's answer and was sure he'd never try the "Rails of

Death". He had no intention of ending up in the emergency room.

"What do you wanna do now? You wanna go see if the bum's asleep? First one to land a backside 360 over him wins." David joked.

"That's the last thing we need. Let's skate to the Courthouse. There's lots of killer stuff on the way," Mike suggested.

Cedric enthusiastically voiced his approval. He was in a hurry to get away from the "Rails" before David dared him to try them. He set his board down and skated in the direction of the courthouse. He was trying his hardest to look cool and collected. Mike and David looked at each other and shared a quiet laugh. They were happy to have made an impression on their friend. Secretly, both of them wished he would have tried at least once.

It was about a mile and half between the Theater and the Courthouse. The boys glided quickly toward their next destination, stopping at intriguing spots to bust moves along the way. Like metal balls in a pinball machine, they bounced from obstacle to obstacle. At one point, Mike and David held wheelies for almost a straight block, lost in the rush of skateboarding, and hypnotized by the perfect combination of concentration, smooth pavement, and speed.

A block later, Mike lagged behind, lost in thoughts of Angela, anxiety creeping into his world. Sailing past a darkened side street his reflections were interrupted by hushed, angry voices. He peered down the block and made out three dark figures threatening someone. He strained to hear their menacing words.

"Where's jur money?" the man closest to the victim demanded. "Give me jur money now mang!"

The victim, a young, small, blonde man insisted, "I don't have any money. The twenty was all I had left. Please let me go."

"Jou want me to put my foot in jur face?" the mugger threatened. "I'm gonna beat jou unless jou give me some money."

With muted whispers, Mike waved his arms frantically and signaled his friends. Seeing his urgency, they rushed to his side. The boys realized what they had come upon when he pointed down the darkened street. They grabbed their boards, summoned their courage and stealthily walked toward the crime. When they were too close to turn back, they spotted a shiny black gun pointed directly at the frightened, cowering victim.

"I don't have time for thees. Give me jur money or I'm gonna put a cap in jou. Got it eh-se?" the mugger yelled violently, his shaking hands wrapped around the gun he held just inches from the small man's face

"Hey dudes, no need for guns," David firmly stated, surprising himself and his friends. "Looks like he doesn't have any money anyways."

The band of criminals was completely startled, not having heard the skaters approaching as they had been completely focused on threatening their prey. They snapped around to face the rescuers. The victim recognized his moment of salvation and ran away as fast as he could, never looking back.

"Mang, eh-se. Did jou guys see what jou jest deed?" asked the main mugger. "He jest took off with our dinero. Maybe we'll jest take jur skateboards. What jou think?"

The thugs angrily nodded their heads in agreement. The gunman put his pistol back in his waistband, but not until he was certain the skaters had taken a good look. They spread out and encircled the boys, corralling them from any chance at escape. Mike glanced at David, who was keeping an eye on the mugger in charge. Cedric and Mike gripped their boards by both trucks, ready for the unexpected. A lesson the boys had long ago learned was now put into action, a board always makes a good shield or weapon.

"Homeless Gang eh-se. Meanest gang in EP. We kill suckers like jou." The hood David was covering was speaking. "Geev us jur skateboards, we'll let jou go no hassle. Else my friend here will have to put a cap in jou. Comprende?" Veins were starting to appear near his temples. The boys' stomachs turned as they understood who they were up against and the seriousness of their confrontation.

In the heat of the threats, Mike managed to make out distant but familiar noises. They were coming in their direction. His ears perked up and he felt an inner peace spreading. As the sounds grew louder, everyone's attention turned toward them. Voices interspersed with the sounds. Not willing to miss his chance, Mike yelled as loud as he could, "Yo, skaters, what's up?!"

A group of five older skateboarders rounded the corner. It was Big Larry and some of his buddies. At six foot three and two hundred and forty pounds, Larry looked more like a college linebacker than a skater. He loved skating downtown after hours when businesses were closed and traffic was minimal. He also had a reputation as someone you shouldn't cross. Cedric's face lit up with relief. He had worked in Larry's shop last summer and knew him well. "Hey Larry! Over here." Cedric yelled.

"Cedric. What's up?" Big Larry called as he approached. He was beginning to understand what was happening. "Who're these guys?"

The hood with the gun lifted his shirt and proudly displayed it.

"Oh, I get it," Larry said, "This is some kind of stick up, right?" Larry and his "old school" friends were an intimidating presence. Despite the severity of their predicament, the boys smiled finding comfort in their numbers.

"Jur friends heer was jest about to geev us theys skateboards. Now maybe we'll have to take jurs also."

Larry's eyes narrowed, turning an ominous shade of blue. "Over my dead body."

"OK eh-se. My compadre can take care of that."

"I'm sure he can," Big Larry said, pulling back a bit. "Let's make this easy for everyone. I'm sure we can work it out."

"Jur boys heer messed up a collection we's making. Geev us fifty dollars and we'll let jou go without shooting jou."

"Fifty dollars!" Mike exclaimed. "How do you think we're going to get fifty dollars?"

"That's the price, eh-se. Or we take jur skateboards," The leader's gaze never left Big Larry's.

Larry glanced at his now somber friends.

Although they had the hoods outnumbered, the great equalizer changed the odds. The last thing he wanted was a one-sided shoot-out on some no-named side street. He pulled a small wad of bills out of his pocket.

"I'll tell you what," he offered, "I've got thirty-five dollars. We'll let you go without fighting. You might shoot one or two of us, but the rest of us will give you the beat down of your lives." Like the resounding silence before the deadly storm, the calm in Big Larry's voice and eyes chilled the thugs' veins and stunned the young skaters who were grateful for their liberator's threatening presence. The boys had witnessed firsthand how Big Larry had earned his reputation. They, like the Homeless Gang, had no doubt the thugs would pay a hefty price for their failure to compromise.

"No one else has money, eh-se?" the main mugger asked shifting his gaze toward the other skaters. Big Larry would not let the moment pass. He stepped up to the punk, "They might, but why don't I give you all I have. Let's leave the others out of it. I'm offering you thirty-five dollars, and absolutely no hassle. We can all get home in one piece if you take it." The punk looked at his friends and then at Big Larry. Without saying a word he reached out and grabbed the money, walking away with his minions in tow. Just like that, it was all over.

The leader looked over his shoulder and called to the group as he left, "If we see jou again, things might be different next time." The underlings laughed and slapped each others' backs as they hustled down the street. "Cap those mothers. See tha look on them?" Their chatter was audible until they rounded the corner at the end of the block.

"Thanks Larry," Cedric sighed heavily, reaching up to pat him on the shoulder and grateful the skirmish had ended without bloodshed. "I thought we were goners."

Mike and David, euphoric and indebted, offered to pay back the money Larry had just lost. He waved them off coolly and set down his board, casually stepping on its tail. Despite his relaxed movements, the relief in Larry's face was evident. "Don't mention it guys. Money can be replaced. You know what's sad? A few years ago I skated with the punk that had the gun. He didn't even recognize me. I'll bet he's a spook."

"What's a spook?" Cedric asked.

"A guy who sniffs paint. They sniff so much it damages their brain and they walk around in a stupor." Larry continued with his bittersweet reminiscence, "That kid used to skate my ramp. He wasn't a bad kid and was actually pretty good. I saw him try a 540 once. He almost made it. I can't believe he hooked up with the Homeless Gang."

"He didn't look like a skater," David exclaimed in disbelief. "He looks like he was born in a gang. Skinny with all those gang symbols tattooed on his arms…"

"His dad was killed when he was eight. I don't think he ever got over it," Big Larry shook his head in a moment of thoughtful reflection. After a short silence, he broke the mood, "Hey, we're heading over to the Abraham Chavez Theater. You guys wanna come?"

Cedric barely glanced at Mike and David and responded too quickly, "No thanks. We just skated there. Gonna head to the Courthouse." He had successfully axed any plans his friends may have entertained to join Big Larry at the "Rails of Death".

"The Courthouse? That's where we're going later. Then across the border."

"Dog Tacos?" Mike asked.

"Yeah. Dog Tacos. I never remember the real name. They're the best!" Larry proclaimed.

"Absolutely the best tacos in the world," Cedric chimed in. "We might see you there."

"Are you guys sure you feel safe? Those were some pretty mean hombres."

"Yeah," Cedric said. "We'll be OK."

"Be careful skating downtown. It can be pretty dangerous, especially for you young dudes. You sure you don't want to skate with us?"

"Thanks, but I think we can make it to the Courthouse OK," Cedric confidently replied, regretting his response the minute he said it. Mike and David quietly exchanged glances and wished Cedric had taken the offer. None of the friends had completely recovered from their encounter with the notorious and deadly local gang. Protecting their machismo and prevented by their egos from retracting Cedric's statement, they held to their charade of bravery.

"Well then. Stay alert. Remember, danger lurks everywhere," Larry waved as he pushed his board. His friends followed his lead.

The boys helplessly watched Big Larry and his crew skate out of sight. Mike got on his board and pushed in the opposite direction. Their destination was still over a mile away. New danger lurked around every corner. This time the boys didn't stop and skate curbs or ledges, they skated fast and kept up the pace. They knew they'd be safe in the shadows of the justice center comprised of the courthouse, jail and police station.

The skaters flew past ominous shadows of dark storefronts and office buildings. Occasionally, they became peripherally aware of a tiny restaurant or bar and grill tucked into the corner of a building. The aromas and sounds they emitted serving as proof that they were surrounded by civilization. Soon, the darkness would be replaced by the well-lit streets of the city's heart. Mike kept his pace as they entered the plaza and sped past the idling buses.

The streets leading to the jail and police station were void of interesting and challenging obstacles. Contrastingly, the block on which the Courthouse sat was a veritable gold mine. They came upon different sized sets of stairs, sweet handrails, grindable marble ledges and freshly painted curbs. Despite the nighttime traffic, this spot was the highlight of the night's skating.

The three teenagers shredded with reckless abandon, popping ollies off of and onto everything in sight. Mike kickflipped off of a three-foot high ledge, caught the board with his feet and landed with a nice smack of the wheels and no body jerk, just fluid motion. After thirty minutes of unspoken competition, Cedric announced it was nine and time to go to Mexico.

Mike opted for one more trick. He climbed on top of a tall ledge and tossed his board under his front foot. Pushing as hard as he could, he skated fast toward the lip, popping an ollie and jumping down to the sidewalk eight feet below. He landed solid and rolled away smooth and fast, turning his board sideways in a screeching powerslide and stopping inches from the trafficked street. An old man in a small sedan waiting at the light hit his horn in a reflexive response. Mouth agape he sat in surprise and disbelief at the kid who had suddenly dropped from the sky and barreled toward him.

It was a spectacular jump and a dramatic ending to their session. David and Cedric had watched, open-mouthed as the pilot flew through the night air. To make it more magnificent, a street lamp purposefully haloed his silhouette as he floated for an inordinate amount of time above the city below. It was an amazing display of talent and skill, edgy, live art in motion. His ollie was as awesome and beautiful as the Cassimus photos or Steadman portraits that hung in Larry's shop, only this was better because it was live, real-time, make it or break it.

After the excitement and well-deserved praise, they ended Phase One of their itinerary. Phase Two, Dog Tacos, was next on their agenda. Cedric took the lead, setting a brisk pace toward Stanton Street where the bridges joining the "Twin Sisters" rose above the Rio Grande River. They opted for the Santa Fe Street bridge because it crossed directly into the bustling Juarez tourist district, where the streets and sidewalks were so old and cracked that it would be impossible to skate.

Mike spotted the bridge from several blocks away, the U.S. and Mexican flags flying high over it. The closer they got, the more alive the city streets became. Large numbers of Mexican nationals were milling about in front of little stores and bus stops that lined the street, enjoying Friday night in the United States.

One side of the bridge allowed one-way traffic and pedestrians to cross into Mexico. Travelers were awarded swift passage. In stark contrast, on the other side, entry was extremely delayed. Protecting the border were meticulous agents searching for guns, smugglees, drugs and other contraband. Tired passengers impatiently sat in overheated cars waiting for hours in hope that they would soon be admitted to America. The majority of cars on the bridge carried American tourists who were usually flagged in without incident. A suspicious passenger or car would be directed into a separate designated area for further investigation. Tonight, the secondary inspection spots were full. Armed agents and drug-sniffing dogs thoroughly scrutinized these vehicles and their passengers. Occasionally, a commotion would ensue, a car would be impounded and the travelers handcuffed. Those who made it through without incident would stare out their windows as they safely crossed into El Paso, captivated by the action on the border.

Out on the bridge, in the stale air of stalled traffic and toxic fumes, vendors from Mexico walked between the rows of cars waiting to get into America. The vendors sold gum, candies, puppets on strings, and other small items. Most of them were dark, sun-scarred Mexican or Indian children between five and ten years old carrying colorful inventory that sharply contrasted against their skin. These small children evoked the most empathy from the rich Americans. Consequently, they were the most successful at selling their wares. Throughout the night, the child vendors would deposit their proceeds with their handlers, old men and women who also worked the bridge selling cigarettes or begging for alms. Despite the tattered clothes and worn out shoes, it was a thriving business.

The women always had a baby in tow. It was said most of the little ones did not belong to them but were mere props in their ruse to con sympathetic tourists into readily parting with their dollars. It was rumored the children were stolen and sold on the black market once they had outgrown their usefulness. Such tales, however, did not stop the Americans from contributing; feeling satisfied they had helped someone less fortunate.

The black-market vendors were not the only

ones working the bridge. Salesmen acting on their own behalf, sole proprietors, were older, slower and easier to spot. They shot angry looks at the younger, more aggressive child vendors who swarmed back and forth between the rows of cars, picking most of the sales clean before the sole proprietors could arrive. As a result, most of these older salesmen stayed toward the end of the lines, hoping to do business without having to fight the swarms of children selling closer to the American checkpoint.

At the pedestrian gate heading one-way into Mexico, the skaters waited in a short line to pay their entry fare and pass through turnstiles that opened onto the pathway across the bridge. Each boy gave the attendant 40 cents, the price required for admission. They pushed through the turnstiles and were immediately caught in a herd of people. Like wildebeest searching for greener pastures, the boys joined the migration.

Most Friday evenings, the Mexican side of the bridge was teeming with pedestrians. Families holding shopping bags, maids, laborers, and American tourists were all part of the familiar scene. The skaters reached the middle of the bridge where the actual border was marked with a plaque. The crowds pushed them past the marker and toward the main street ahead. Juarez was crowded and bustling with all shapes and forms of human life. Rancheros, working girls, businessmen and beggars all walked together along the dirty and broken sidewalks, a collision of cultures highlighted under the eerie glow of the neon signs.

A couple of GIs on leave from Fort Bliss hooted and ran through the crowd rushing toward Mexico as fast as they could, the excitement of cheap liquor and easy girls drawing them like metal to magnets. At the end of the night, some of these same GIs would get into brawls at the discos and be escorted into El Paso by the military police. As they passed Mike, one of the soldiers accidentally knocked his board down. Mike stopped in the moving mass to retrieve it but was knocked to his knees by another overeager GI. David extended his hand and pulled Mike back to safety, "Careful, bro! Don't want to lose you."

"Thanks D" Mike said shakily.

Oblivious to the fall, Cedric continued with the flow, crossing into Juarez first. Looking back, he waited for his friends to catch up. He had a big grin. "Don't you love this?" Cedric shouted as they got close, opening his arms wide in a Christ-like fashion.

"Man. This is insane," David yelled back. "I've never seen so many people. Where do they all come from?"

"It's just getting started," Cedric laughed. "More will come when the bars close in El Paso. It'll really get crazy."

"You mean this isn't crazy?" Mike shrugged his shoulders and looked around.

"Hey, you want to get a drink at the Kentucky Club? The Margarita was invented there." Cedric had no qualms in asking, as the legal drinking age was a fuzzy topic and children as young as 13 were often served beer.

"Nah, let's just go to Dog Tacos." David had no intention of barhopping in Juarez. Kids were sometimes kidnapped or ended up in Mexican jails and he did not want to take that kind of risk.

Mike shook his head in agreement, "Let's eat

these freaky tacos!" He was caught up in the strangeness of the city. Cars and people danced with each other along the main street, moving in quick spasms of chaotic unison. Lights from cabs, bars, and bouncers stabbed the darkness, all searching for the same prey, the American tourist. Mike had never seen such a radical metamorphosis. He lived less than five miles away from where he stood, yet it was an entirely different world.

"It's up ahead about four blocks," Cedric pointed in the direction he was heading. Mike surveyed the sidewalks and streets, deciding there must be a few thousand noisy people crammed into that short four-block distance. Claustrophobia set in as he followed Cedric who had disappeared into the deafening mob.

"Get on the street!" Cedric shouted back. "It's faster." Avoiding the hordes standing in line for their turn to pay the cover charge and dance under the strobe lights that flashed to the beat, the skaters jumped onto the avenue and hugged the parked cars as they made their way forward. Their new path facilitated their speedy movement through the pack.

Two blocks later, Cedric slowed as Mike and David caught up. He steered them onto the sidewalk again. Near the end of the block, sandwiched between a pharmacy and a bank, he pointed up at a red and blue sign announcing "Club Kentucky". The arched window displayed another sign, "The Kentucky Club" to notify American patrons that this was in fact the world famous bar in which celebrities like James Dean, Sammy Davis, Jr., and Nat King Cole had hung out.

"You sure you don't want go in?" Cedric gave his friends another shot.

"Naw, let's get tacos," David replied. "We've still got a party."

"Yeah," Mike added. "Anyway, you shouldn't drink on an empty stomach."

"That's what I'm talking about. Better buzz," Cedric laughed as he passed the bar full of teenagers and bikers, a look of longing on his face. "No worries. We're almost there." He led his friends onward.

Like a tree branch swinging toward an unsuspecting victim, a taxi driver leaned in as the boys passed and sneered, "What jou want? Girls? Drugs? I geet jou drugs and girls if jou want. Come on. Where jou want me to take jou? I know all the best whorehouses in Juarez."

Cedric protectively pushed his buddies past the wannabe-concierge. "Don't go anywhere with these guys. They're shiftless and will scam your money." His wise words went unchallenged. They agreeably followed Cedric's commands and willfully continued in his chosen direction.

A few steps into the next block, a gang of seven small, dirty and scruffy street kids, orphans in the large, immoral city, circled the boys. Mike couldn't help but empathize with the urchins. "Being homeless would've sucked," he thought, grateful for the safe haven his grandmother provided. The oldest orphan stepped up to Cedric, "Skateboards. Let me try jur skateboards?" He had an innocent childlike expression on his face.

Cedric laughed, "No skateboarding. Con permiso." He tried to pass, but the kids blocked him and grabbed at his board. Cedric yanked it out of reach and roughly pushed the largest boy away. In a last ditch attempt, the big orphan lunged up and clutched the board. A tug-of-war ensued but the boy was no match for Cedric's teenage strength. With a last jerk, Cedric freed the board and sent the orphan sprawling to the ground.

Signaling his friends to follow, Cedric moved quickly to the next street corner and took a right. Mike and David stayed close to Cedric, shocked by his display of callousness toward the homeless, vulnerable strays. The gang of kids moved on to a different target, not daring to follow the teenager who had knocked down their leader.

Chapter

6

Across the street, in the middle of the block, embedded in an old one-and-a-half story building was a lone bright orange garage door that opened onto the sidewalk. Cedric walked toward it briskly. Mike and David followed.

As they neared the building, Mike's senses zeroed in on the smell of grilling meat. He instantly salivated while deeply inhaling the savory, aromatic smoke wafting out of the building's chimney. He could see several people standing around inside the tiny space while the smoke rose through a ventilation hood in the front right corner. A few individuals had their backs to the door, shoulders hunched and elbows bent as if eating a cob of corn. The rest were staring at the show being performed by the two cooks. It was a strange congregation of nighttime cohorts, all brought together to pay homage to the almighty taco.

When they were almost to the garage door, a very tall, large man wearing a plaid cotton shirt, blue jeans, grey cowboy boots and a straw cowboy hat caught Mike's attention. The rancher hunched over the plate of tacos he held in one hand while his other tightly held a tiny taco. Every time he took a bite he'd hunch even more over the plate. Mike swore he even heard the man let out a snort.

This hole in the wall, this crowded little space, this converted little one-car garage was the much-heralded Dog Tacos. Mike didn't understand why

Cedric would rant and rave about a place so small and on such a dark and dirty side street.

That's when he heard it. The sound made Mike's stomach tense. He wanted to turn and run, but instead he hurriedly walked back out onto the street and turned, looking upward at the building.

"Hey, where are you going Mike?" asked Cedric. "We're here. Let's order some food."

Along the top of the building above Dog Tacos was a chain link fence. Behind it were three very large German Shepherds barking wildly at Mike below. His mouth dropped open and his face turned a pale shade of green.

"What's that?" Mike asked seriously, trying to stop the gag reflexes in his throat while pointing to the noisy, vicious dogs on the roof. "This isn't a reality show stunt, is it? I don't want to eat someone's dog. Let's go somewhere else." In repulsed dismay, he backed out farther into the street.

Cedric chuckled as David walked over, still slightly confused. Mike became more agitated over the German Shepherds, causing Cedric to convulse in laughter, tears streaming down his cheeks.

Mike stood in the middle of the street, red faced and pointing at the dogs. David started laughing once he understood. A few of the patrons looked out at the scene, momentarily confused. Those who caught on, quickly shrugged their shoulders and returned to their meals.

Mike started walking away from the taco shack toward the main street. David and Cedric chased after him, catching up before he could reach the end

of the block. Cedric explained the dogs belonged to
the owner of the restaurant.

"Big Larry nicknamed it Dog Tacos because of
those three German Shepherds," he continued. "My
first time I also noticed the dogs on the roof. It's
weird, they're right above the taco stand. Check out
the sign - El Taquito Mexicano. These are some of
the best tacos you'll find in Juarez. Probably in all of
Mexico, or anywhere."

"What kind of meat are they made of?" Mike
asked suspiciously, still visibly disturbed.

"Some kind of pork. You know, like the best
cut, the shoulder or something. Not only are the
tacos good, wait 'til you see the show. The tortilla
lady says they've been here for over 35 years! Come
on dude. Let's go back in." Cedric was talking fast
and trying everything he could to get Mike inside.
He knew he'd fall in love once he gave them a try.

"What do you think, David? I'll go in if you go
in," Mike said cautiously; he still hadn't quite made
up his mind.

"Of course I wanna go in!" David exclaimed.
"Did you see the people eating in there? They were
pigging out. C'mon, let's go in!"

The boys walked back to the little restaurant,
making it all the way inside this time. Cedric placed
their order with the cooks as they entered: sodas and
an order of tacos for each. He didn't bother getting
Mike and David's input. The bright red and yellow
menu board above the condiments bar listed 3
items: "Orden $20", "Media Orden $10", and
"Sodas $8". The English translation was listed next
to each: "Order $1.80", Half Order $0.90", and
"Sodas $0.70".

A couple of people got up to leave and the boys quickly grabbed their barstools, tucking their skateboards under the shelf that ran along the wall opposite the grill and functioned as a counter. Several small tables, each capable of snuggly seating four average-sized diners, lined the wall behind the grill. In all, Dog Tacos could seat a maximum of 20. Currently, there were 11 customers, including the boys. It was still fairly crowded, considering its size.

Under the menu board was a clean, well-stocked condiments bar. It was filled with crushed ice and stainless steel bowls. Each bowl was spotless and had a glass cover and serving spoon or fork. They contained freshly chopped onions, cilantro, jalapenos, lime wedges and a variety of salsas. An employee was busy maintaining the sparkle of the area and restocking the napkin holders. At the back of the restaurant, set into the bright orange wall, was a very clean, large double-glass door refrigerator containing a wide variety of Mexican sodas in old-fashioned glass bottles.

Cedric grabbed a lemon-lime soda and David an orange. Mike was overwhelmed with the choices. Root beer, pineapple, apple, cola... He finally slid open the door, choosing pineapple. The boys looked back at the small, gnarled chefs, a man and a woman. The lady had taken twelve little balls of masa from her bowl. She flattened them and placed them on the grill. As the little tortillas cooked she'd flip them with her bare hands. The man took a large butcher knife and shaved small slices from the slab of meat cooking on the vertical grill.

The tortilla maker then placed the cooked tortillas in paper boats and handed them to the meat chef. He filled them with pieces of grilled meat and, slid each of them a full order of four tiny tacos.

"There are some salsas at the counter and some jalapeños, pickled onions and cilantro," Cedric instructed. "They're super good with onion and cilantro. I like mine with salsa also, especially the green tomatillo avocado. It's a little milder than the rest, but man its good. Careful though 'cause it's still pretty hot."

Mike and David reviewed and assessed the selection. They matched the colorful décor. Bright green tomatillo, deep red habanero, dark brown chipotle. The once white onions were sliced small and had a pinkish color from soaking in red wine vinegar. Next to the onions was a bowl of fresh green cilantro leaves, minced for maximum flavor and coverage. Small slices of jalapeños and crispy orange carrot slices floated in the last bowl.

Mike piled on the tomatillo salsa with some onion and cilantro, squeezing a little lime and sprinkling some salt on top. He took his first bite as David put some habanero salsa on his. Cedric sat back to watch their expressions. Mike's first bite was hot and good. He looked at Cedric, nodded his head and raised his eyebrows. The meat was cooked perfectly and the fresh salsa and crisp onion complimented each bite. He felt an instant stinging from the chile, but it was doable. It was so unbelievably good that Mike disregarded the increasing discomfort and continued to eat, drying his already sweaty forehead with his napkin.

"Dude, these tacos are great. They're probably the best I've ever had. How much do I owe you?" Mike was in a much better mood now.

"Two-fifty. Same for you David."

"Man, we'd pay at least five dollars for that in El Paso," Mike said as David took his first bite. "And that's without the soda."

"Diiiaaammnn," David rubbed his stomach as he spoke, "This is a good taco. No, this is a great taco." He grinned and sunk his teeth into another bite.

Cedric smiled. "See guys, don't you think it was worth the trip?"

Mike and David didn't answer. They were hunched over their plates, devouring their food, and could only nod their heads in consensus. By the time Cedric got to his first bite, Mike and David were on their last. The tacos were excellent, but they were tiny. In fact, they were the smallest Mike had ever seen or eaten. They were ready for round two, but waited patiently for Cedric to finish.

"Well, what do you think?" asked Cedric. "Were the tacos good enough to compete with the almighty Chico's?"

Mike smiled and nodded his approval. He panted a couple of times, trying to cool the burning sensation in his mouth. He desperately took another swig of his soda, but it did nothing more than momentarily cool him. "I have to admit these are the best. I could eat these all night."

"I once saw a guy eat 24, six orders! The cooks said he was a famous bullfighter from Tijuana who eats here every year when he fights in Juarez. They said every time he comes, he orders 24 tacos and eats them all. Speaking of orders, you guys ready for round two?" Cedric asked.

"I'll take two orders this time and another soda," Mike replied quickly. He had found a place to rival the great Chico's Tacos, something he'd never have considered before tonight.

"Me too. Two more orders and a drink," David chimed in. "These are the best. We'll have to come here again soon," he enthusiastically suggested as he reactively chugged big gulps of his cool soda. The back of his neck and forehead were glistening with sweat from the hot habanero salsa.

The cooks started their show for the next round of tacos. Masa flattened and cooked, meat shaved, tacos ready. Soon, the boys had their second and third full orders. Mike thought the tomatillo chile was very tasty, so he spooned it on in excess. He knew it was hot but it was so good. It was the salsa that brought the tacos to life. They hopped with the zest of the chile and snapped with the crisp freshness of the onions and cilantro. The lime juice added another dimension of taste.

Mike bit a taco drenched in salsa. The sweet heat of the jalapeño bit his lips and tongue, burning him like a flame burns a moth, and just like the moth returns to the flame, burn after burn, Mike returned to the chile, until all his tacos were gone.

"This green sauce is some hot stuff," cried Mike after his last bite. He was huffing repeatedly and sweat was pouring down his face. "I'm burning up. Nothing's helping!" The collar on his shirt was soaked with sweat. He felt like his head was melting.

David and Cedric laughed at Mike's salsa overdose, red, sweaty face and neck. Of course, they also were sweating like crazy, but hadn't eaten enough chile to reach the agitated state their friend was in. The cooks and customers focused their attention on the boys, amused at the red faced kid who was huffing and puffing, dripping sweat, and gulping the last of his second pineapple soda.

"All they have here are sodas Mike. On the corner they sell that rice milk, horchata. It'll get rid of the burn. Do you want to get some of that?" To Mike's relief, Cedric was a wealth of information regarding Juarez. He shook his head yes and grabbed his skateboard. Cedric called "Adios" to the still smiling cooks and followed his friends out into the night air. A loud wave of laughter and hoots erupted inside Dog Tacos as they left.

"Let's grab... some horchata," huffed Mike as he tried to inhale and exhale enough air to regulate the flaming heat inside his mouth. "I need... to drink... something... that will... provide me... relief quick. I'm burning up." His eyes were becoming bloodshot. He needed something cool and soothing, fast. David and Cedric laughed as they all ran to the vendor with the magic elixir. Mike ordered a large drink and greedily drank from it as soon as the vendor gave him his glass. Droplets ran down his chin as he chugged over and over.

"Aaaahhhh," Mike sighed as the coolness of the drink relieved the hot, throbbing burn. As he chugged, his friends each bought a glass. They were also victims of the hot chile and needed something soothing. The vendor was amused by Mike's greedy gulping. He had no idea the boy had just overdosed on salsa and was in need of liquid salvation.

Looking at David and Cedric, he rolled his eyes, pointed to his ear and circled his finger, indicating he believed Mike was loco. The boys cracked into laughter again. Cedric explained they had just been at El Taquito Mexicano. The salesman, having eaten there before, nodded his understanding and offered to refill Mike's glass.

"Gratis. Por nada, por nada," the Elixir Salesman said, grinning broadly and waving his hand in the air.

Mike was grateful for the generous refill of horchata. Afterward, he tipped the vendor three dollars, a dollar more than the price of the drink. The vendor displayed a mouthful of huge, white teeth as he waved good-bye to the boys and shouted after them, "Buenas noches! Buenas noches, Señores!"

"Man that was an experience! Now, I really feel like skating," laughed Mike. "All that chile has got my testosterone pumping. I'm ready to dominate the Rails of Death!"

"What about the party? I thought we were going there," David asked. "I'm supposed to meet Natassia. You know, we're probably going to take a little walk, and talk a little talk. Who knows where it could lead from there." He slapped Mike on the back and pulled him in close. Mike pulled away and brushed off his sleeve in mock indignation.

"Come on, Mike," Cedric said. "There'll be a couple of kegs and lots of girls! You've got to come with us. It's one of the year's best parties."

"That's cool. I'll probably skate around outside while you guys go in. Don't worry about me." Mike wanted to date Angela and was more interested in skating than meeting other girls. Besides, everyone would be drinking and Mike didn't want to deal with it.

The boys started crossing the bridge back to El Paso, boards in hand. The pedestrians consisted mostly of GIs and high-schoolers. The majority of them were feeling the effects of the watered down alcohol consumed in the Mexican bars. Up ahead, one group of revelers was walking three abreast with their arms around one another, singing Christmas songs in the middle of May.

Every ten or twenty feet on the Mexican side of the border, the boys sidestepped persistent beggars. Most of them were women and children from the Tarahumara tribe. They were easy to spot because they were shorter and darker than most Mexicans, and had uniquely round faces that resembled the Inuit from Alaska. The women wore layers of colorful skirts so they could conveniently remove the top layer to the inside once it was soiled.

Mike knew all about the Tarahumara from his grandmother who had played with them as a child in Creel. Oftentimes, she ran through their cornfields grown in terraces carved into the side of the Sierra Madre mountains. Although she was welcomed into their homes and gardens, her Indian friends were ostracized in certain parts of town. Grandma told him of visiting Copper Canyon, home of the Tarahumara tribe. She would proudly tell him the entire region had more than twenty canyons and that five of them were deeper and longer than the Grand Canyon.

Mike shared these stories with his companions. "They're known as the world's best distance runners. She always talks about a Tarahumara friend whose dad belonged to a hunting party. They chased wild game, sometimes for days, until their prey collapsed from exhaustion!"

"Why would they come here?" Cedric asked. "Copper Canyon sounds awesome."

"They're escaping the cartels," Mike said. "You rarely see the men in Juarez because they're either dead or involved with drugs."

His parents had taken him to Copper Canyon when he was five. He vaguely remembered how beautiful it was but clearly recalled the Tarahumaras' dignity - they didn't look discarded like the beggars on the bridge. Equally ingrained in his memory were the stoned-out teenagers with their 4X4s and AK-47s, the result of the drug trade infiltrating their remote homeland. They were a stark contrast to their elders who still depended on the land for their livelihood.

His reflections reminded him of the beautiful and interesting places they visited as a family. His parents thoroughly enjoyed life and welcomed new experiences with open arms. He was lucky to have had them.

His favorite memory was of a trip to Hatch, New Mexico. His dad loved chile and went to the Hatch Chile Festival every August. On this particular trip, he had determined Mike was six and old enough to spend a hot, miserable day at a dusty field in the middle of nowhere.

The festival didn't look like much from a distance - Mike wasn't feeling it. Once there, however, the live bands, dancing, food, crafts and fun quickly drew him in. Everywhere they went green chiles were roasting and fresh produce was on display. It was a land of plenty. Mike danced with his mom, ate hot food and sweet deserts until he thought he could eat no more. His father spent most of his time bartering with the farmers until they reached an acceptable price. Mike proudly helped his dad carry the heavy bags of produce back to the car.

At the end of the day, his dad proudly showed the family his booty: two large pungent fifty pound burlap bags of onions, a fifty pound bag of roasted chiles and five watermelons. Back in El Paso he stopped at a grocery store and went in alone. He came out loaded with several bags of groceries. At home, he made chile con queso with the Hatch produce, and a delicious sweet watermelon drink that he displayed in a large five-gallon glass jar, much like the one the elixir salesman used for his horchata. While his mom made fresh tortillas and pico de gallo in the kitchen, his father fired up the grill for fajitas and began calling family and friends to come over and enjoy the fruits of their labor.

This feast was an event he would remember the rest of his life. Every family that came was treated to a bag of roasted chiles and a bag of onions to take home after the fiesta. The get-together lasted until early the next morning, when Uncle Ralph and his then-girlfriend Sonia finally left after breakfast.

That day Mike felt completely safe and secure, his parents were in charge of their destiny. Little did he know he only had three more years with them. His parents always shared with others and took special care to include everyone. His bittersweet memories were beginning to tear him.

Near the middle, Cedric pointed at a bunch of stickers stuck high on the light posts that lined the bridge. The Reptile Skateboards stickers were at least fifteen feet up on the posts. They were faded from the sun and looked to be fairly old.

"Cool!" Mike shouted excitedly. "I wonder how those got there!" They were all pondering the mystery when Mike suddenly and unexpectedly burped loudly. The boys laughed.

"Dog Tacos! That's a good tasting burp," Mike exclaimed. "Even if it is dog meat..."

"Come on! Beer and women are waiting for us!" Cedric urged, cutting Mike off.

Chapter
7

The boys walked faster on the downhill half of the bridge. Ahead, bright lights lit up the Border Patrol station. Their power so strong it looked like high noon.

Lines of cars created hot breezes of wilted exhaust fumes. The occasional tourist beckoned the salesman of their choice. The most popular offerings were cellophane-wrapped Chiclets and tubes of burnt toffee peanuts. Tireless vendors hawking their wares braved the clouds of carbon monoxide to make their sales.

Closer to the American entry point, large signs warned pedestrians to throw away illegal paraphernalia in the attached receptacle or risk going to jail. Mike wanted to look inside, his imagination ran wild, but the mailbox shape and the watchful eye of the agents precluded him from satisfying his curiosity.

About 100 feet from the entry point, the boys heard loud running and yelling. They turned and saw four large figures barreling toward them. This time, Mike quickly stepped aside, allowing them to blow right past as they yelled in unison, "Hoo-Rah! Hoo-Rah!"

Mike laughed commenting, "Must be GIs from Fort Bliss on weekend leave."

David added, "One time at the Worm, I met this GI named Joaquin. He was from California and could skate anything - he was schooled by some pros."

"I didn't think GIs skated," Cedric commented.

"They're at the Worm all the time. They're not just agents of death, you know," David continued as they reached the Border Patrol building.

On weekdays, lines of people blocks long would wait to declare their citizenship before trained agents who scrutinized the masses. At ten o'clock on a Friday night, the line was almost non-existent. There were about 15 people entering the double doors ahead of the boys.

Inside the station, single file lines led to three turnstiles with inspectors at the helm. The boys got into the same line. The uniformed agent wore mirrored sunglasses even though they were indoors at night. He was about six feet tall and had a belly that hung well over his belt buckle. With his handlebar mustache and permanent scowl, he was an intimidating sight.

"Watchyall's citizenship son?" the inspector questioned Cedric, snarling and sniffing in the direction of his skateboard.

"American," Cedric looked a little tense under the scrutiny.

"Whastup with the contraption there son?" the inspector genuinely looked perplexed.

"We took our boards with us sir. We skated around town before we went into Mexico."

The agent impatiently waved him through, eyeing the skateboard as Cedric passed.

"How bout choo?" he menacingly stared at David. "Whaz yur nationality son?"

"American," David replied.

"Are ya bringin anything back from Mezco?" the inspector continued, slightly raising his eyebrows. "You don't got no drugs or paraphernalia on you, do you?"

"No sir."

"How about pills or alcohol? Got any of them?"

"No sir."

"Whut wuz your business in Mezco?"

"We went to eat tacos sir."

"On them rollamajigees?" he pointed at David's skateboard. "You didn't harass the poor citizens of Juarez on those did ya son?"

"We didn't skate over there, we carried our boards sir."

"Yep, that's smart of you. OK, you can pass," he waved David through, his face showing signs of amusement.

"Citizenship?" queried the inspector.

"Italian," joked Mike, believing the officer would find him equally amusing and oblivious to the seriousness of the question posed.

"Papers?" he held out his hand, his face showing no sign of humor or emotion.

"I don't have any papers," Mike shrugged.

"You need to have papers to come into this man's America, Vinny," the inspector's face tensed.

"I was just joking sir. Really, I'm an American citizen."

"Then why'd ya say ya wuz I-talian? Are you some kind of wise ass or somethin?"

"I was just joking sir. I'm sorry." Mike pleaded regretfully.

The inspector's face reddened as he hovered over Mike. "Whut's funny about that son? Don't see nobody laughing none, do ya? You could be a damned terrorist for all I know boy. Do you want to spend the night in a cell until we can prove your citizenship?"

"No sir," Mike said lowering his head.

"Ya know them terrorists and drug dealers lie about their nationality. How do I know you're not one of them? This is serious business you know."

"I'm sorry sir. I'm an American citizen. I shouldn't have said I was Italian."

"I don't unnerstan why you'd say you wuz I-talian when you an American. It doesn't make sense son. You sit over there until we decide what to do with you."

The red-faced inspector relieved his turnstile and made a call on his radio. Soon, two customs agents emerged from a nearby room and conferred with the inspector. The three men walked toward Mike.

"Son, you're gonna have to go with these gentlemen. What you did is a Federal o-fense and you are currently a threat to our borders, ya unnerstan?"

The two agents each took an arm, leading Mike into an interrogation room. The door made a booming noise as it slammed behind them. David and Cedric were left standing in the station, looking at each other, shoulders shrugged.

They had watched the entire spectacle open-mouthed, never having seen anyone detained at the border and having no idea of what to do. There were some chairs in a waiting area, so they went over and sat. Cedric put his skateboard on the ground, placing his feet on top, and rolling it side to side, his knees rocking in the opposite direction of the board.

"What do you think is going to happen?" David asked.

"They'll probably yell at him a lot. We could be here a while," Cedric sighed.

"How do you know?"

"I don't. I'm only guessing. He shouldn't have done that," Cedric said. "Hey, how come Mike doesn't want to go to the party tonight? It's gonna be a blast."

"Yeah, I can't wait. I'm not sure if you know but his mom and dad were killed by a drunk driver when he was nine. He doesn't drink because of that. Alcohol really bothers him."

"Man, I didn't know that. Now I'm sorry I pushed him. I had no idea."

"Sometimes he has a real hard time dealing with it. He sees all drunks as potential killers. I'd probably be the same way if it had been my parents. It's gotta be rough."

David sounded like a big brother. At that moment, he felt like one too. Mike had been his best friend for as long as he could remember. He wished he could get him out of the jam, but all he could do was wait.

Inside the interrogation room the conversation wasn't going well. Mike was sitting on one side of a cheap folding table, the two agents sat on the other with a light shining directly in Mike's face.

One agent was a little over six feet tall. He was sunburned and his dark hair was cropped in a perfect flattop. The other was much shorter and had a weightlifter's build. His wrists were the size of Mike's knees.

The tall agent stood and leaned over the table. His brows met in the middle, creating one furry "V" above his nose. Weird mutant hairs sprouted out of his face. Mike wondered why he didn't trim them.

"You think we're stupid? How'd you like to see how stupid we can be? Maybe we should strip search you or lock you up and deport you back to Mexico, or better yet, how about Italy?"

"I'm sorry sir," Mike said, his body slumped in his chair. "It was a big mistake and I'll never do it again, I swear."

He wished he had just kept his mouth shut. Why did he have to get smart with the inspector? He wondered how long they were going to detain him. Were they going to call his grandmother? Were David and Cedric going to wait?

The shorter agent shifted in his chair and fixed his stare on Mike long and hard. "We need a name and number son," the short agent finally said. "Who can we call to come pick you up?"

"I live with my grandmother. Does she really have to come down here? She's pretty old and it's hard for her to get around. She goes everywhere on the bus and someone else would have to drive her."

"I tell you what, if your grandmother says it's alright, we'll let you go. How's that sound?" The tall agent tried to be friendlier this time.

"I guess that would be good," Mike said, his tension fading slightly.

"What do you mean 'I guess?' We can always hold you for the night," snapped the short agent.

"Yes, I mean yes sir," Mike responded quickly.

"OK then, we'll need your grandmother's name, address and phone number," the agent shoved a pen at him.

"Her name is Alice Rodriguez," Mike said as he wrote her information.

"OK, we'll be back."

As the agents opened the door, Mike saw a clock on the wall - it was eleven-thirty. He had been in there for an hour and fifteen minutes. He hoped his friends had gone to the party without him. It would be nearly over by this time.

Several minutes turned into many. Thirty minutes passed before the door opened again. The two agents were accompanied by an older man in a brown leisure suit. They all stood at the table facing Mike. The older man spoke first.

"Hello Mike. My name is Byron Brandon and I am the director of this U.S. Customs station. My agents here tell me you fraudulently declared your citizenship when returning from Mexico. Is that correct?"

"Yes sir it is. I'm very sorry. It was just a bad joke."

"You're right about that," he said. "It was a joke that could've landed you in prison, a federal prison. You're lucky you got these two fine agents working your case. Other officers might have just sent you back to Mexico or arrested you."

Director Brandon walked around the table. Looking down at the boy, he smiled and squeezed his shoulder. "Your grandmother is a very nice lady. She said you are an outstanding young man and we can be sure you'll never misrepresent your nationality at a U.S. Customs checkpoint again. Is that so?"

"Yes sir," Mike stammered, "I didn't realize the seriousness of my actions then, but I sure do now. I'm sorry I caused all this trouble. I really am."

"OK, Mike," he said, "We're going to let you go, but if we see you at the border again, what are you going to tell us when we ask you to declare your citizenship?"

"I'm an American citizen," Mike said.

"OK. You take care Mike and remember that some jokes can get you in serious trouble. I never want to see you in my interrogation room again. Do you understand me?"

Mike nodded in the affirmative. "Yes sir."

Director Brandon patted him on the back and returned his skateboard, pointing him to the door that led back into the station's lobby. "You get going. Your grandmother's worried."

When he walked through the doors, the clock read twelve twenty-four. Mike quickly spotted his sleeping friends. David sat with his feet on his board, positioned to skate. Occasionally, his board would roll a little to the right or left and he would stir. Cedric lay uncomfortably across three chairs, legs woven through the arms. Despite his awkward position, he was deep asleep and snoring.

"Hey guys wake up," Mike said. "They finally let me go."

Cedric stirred and grumbled, "Don't wake me. I just fell asleep. Wake me up just before school starts."

Mike stifled a laugh and grabbed Cedric's shoulder, rocking it gently. "Time to get up Cedric."

David heard Mike and rubbed the sleep out of his eyes. "He's a heavy sleeper, but this always works."

"Blam!" David whacked the tail of his board on the ground. One of the inspectors looked up, startled by the sound, and glared at him. "Keep it down over there boys. This isn't a playground."

"Sorry. My bad."

Cedric sat up and looked around. He was a little dazed, but quickly gathered his wits and glared at David.

"What was that for?" Cedric asked as he jabbed David in the arm. "I was sleeping so good. Victoria in History was laughing at all my jokes."

"Come on. They're done with Mike. Let's go home."

"What about the party?" asked Cedric.

"It's after midnight. The party'll be over before we get there," David replied. "Let's skate to the bus stop and head home."

"That won't work," Cedric stated.

"Why not? It's only about six blocks to the plaza."

"All the buses stop running at midnight. It's already too late. We're doomed," Cedric said imitating Chuckie from Rug Rats. Mike and David laughed uneasily.

The three boys stood outside the customs station trying to regroup. This was a serious setback. They had to pass through gang territory to get home.

Cedric broke the silence, "Why don't we think of our options? We could take a cab or call someone."

"We had planned to skate home from the party," Mike offered. "This is only about two extra miles."

"That's strange logic, but I like it," David agreed. "I seriously doubt that my Mom would want to drive downtown this late."

"It'll be fun," Cedric chimed in.

Trying to sound like his uncle calling military orders, Mike barked, "Fall in. Next stop Raynolds Street."

Mike dropped his board and started pushing. David and Cedric followed his lead. Crouching low, Cedric popped a fat shifty over a soda can.

"Feels good to skate after sleeping on those cheap seats," he said.

"I agree fully Ced. You know this is all your fault, Vinny?" David poked at Mike. "They should have deported you back to Italy so we could have gone to the party. I bet it was rocking."

"Sorry guys … I guarantee that I'll never… get in trouble there again." Mike's voice bumped in rhythm with each push of his board.

In the long stretches between lights, the street became pitch black. It was so dark that Mike couldn't see the ground in front of him. He kept his knees relaxed and loose in case he hit a small rock or hole in the road.

Suddenly, Mike heard a scuff and then a loud slap and grunt. As Mike turned, he heard the screeching of skateboard wheels. It was Cedric sliding sideways toward David, who was sprawled out on the ground. At the last minute, he leapt up and over David before rolling to a stop.

As Cedric bounced up and shook off his roll, David lay groaning. His jeans were ripped and blood was soaking through the shredded denim. The stinging started as soon as he looked down. It felt like he had slid across sandpaper and come to a stop in rubbing alcohol. Dirt, sweat, and blood combined in small streams, running down his legs until he could feel the liquid soak into his socks.

"David, are you all right man?" Mike asked. "That was a pretty bad fall. Your knees look trashed."

"They sting and they're pretty sore. Nothing's broken though, just bloody. What did I hit?"

The boys looked at David's board, which was half in, half out of a big, black pothole at least twelve inches in diameter. The marks left by David's sliding knees and Cedric's wheels were clearly visible. Shards of denim sprinkled the path.

"Looks like you skated into a pothole," Cedric remarked on the obvious. "I'm glad it was you and not me. Are you OK?"

David winced, "It's merely a flesh wound. I'll be OK. Let's try to stay on streets that have lights if we can. How about skating on Alameda or Montana?"

"If we skate up to Montana Street, it will add a half hour or more. Let's take Alameda," Cedric proffered.

"You lead the way," Mike said, "I'm not real familiar with Alameda. Isn't it kind of dangerous over there?"

"Not as dangerous as people say. I have an uncle who lives there and I've never seen any trouble. In fact, the first house I lived in until I was eight was two blocks away. We used to go to stores and restaurants up there all the time and it wasn't bad."

"That's funny," David said, "my dad took us there the other day and it looked like a hell hole. There were junkies and prostitutes everywhere and stores were all boarded up."

"Well what do you guys want, safe and thirty minutes longer or questionable and quicker?" Cedric summarized their options.

"Quicker does sound better," Mike said. "It's probably close to one o'clock and we're still a long way from home. I vote Alameda. My Grandma's worried. Those Border Patrol guys called her while I was being interrogated."

"We better get going. This way," Cedric said leading his friends. "We'll go past the Federal Building and the Old Plantation. That'll get us to Alameda."

"I was there this morning. Well, uh, yesterday," Mike said.

"What were you doing there?" asked Cedric, "You're not on Federal probation are you?"

"Naw," Mike said, "I had to meet with my case worker."

"Oh. Hey, I'm sorry, I didn't know about that. That's got to be hard," Cedric said.

"Yeah, at first it was real hard, but my Grandmother and Uncle are really cool. I'm lucky I have them."

"True that." Cedric turned right and called out, "Let's head this way a block and then turn left on Mills. The streets will be lit up a little better there."

The boys started skating in the direction of Alameda. It was still over a mile away. Once there, they would be able to skate faster because the street was smoother, and the lighting was better.

Under a street light, Mike popped a nice high ollie off a slanted curb and landed several feet out, his wheels rolling smoothly. At the next corner Cedric turned left.

On the side of a dark building the boys saw a girl standing alone. As they approached, they could hear her sniffling and sobbing. She stood about six feet tall, with long, curly blond hair and legs that didn't end. The boys all looked at each other, raised eyebrows but not objections, and rolled toward the damsel in distress.

They were about twenty feet away from the girl when she noticed them. She sobbed harder and waved her hands at them, trying to shoo her would be heroes.

"Are you all right?" Mike called out.

The girl ignored them and hurriedly walked away, her high heels clunking on the cement with each step.

"Wait," David called after her. "Can we help you? We don't want to hurt you."

The girl ran faster toward the end of the block. She took a right and slowed to a walk. The Old Plantation was a few doors down, its neon sign glowing in the late night darkness. The girl walked up to the entrance and went inside.

"Oh man. I'll bet that wasn't a girl. I'll be that was a guy in drag," David wisely concluded as he pushed his board faster. "You never know what you're going to see in El Paso."

Cedric skated a little faster. "Come on. We're not too far from Alameda. We'll be there in a few minutes."

Chapter
8

Cedric maintained his course toward Alameda Street. The roads were lit better but were rougher. Pebbles, broken glass and sand littered large sections of the street, making it risky to skate fast. One false move and they could slide out or, even worse, hit a rock and come to a complete stop, catapulting onto the ground - a painful, abrupt end to their forward momentum.

The boys rolled cautiously, preferring safety to speed, their pushing feet contacting the pavement in steady, rhythmic beats. The hurdles of the terrain dictated their movements. Sometimes they rolled straight, sometimes from side to side and sometimes in sudden jerky motions.

Sounds Mike normally heard, like cars passing and people speaking seemed muted. There was clarity in his thoughts as he merely rode his board – pure unadulterated transportation.

He felt bad his friends had missed one of the biggest parties of the year. Now they were out after midnight, in a bad part of town, without a ride, because of him. He vowed to be more careful in the future.

He dreaded his homecoming. His grandmother didn't get mad often, but when she did the consequences could be demoralizing. Mike was hurt more by her disappointment than her punishment.

He hoped he wouldn't be grounded – he had a date to keep.

"Angela. Tonight." Mike smiled to himself.

"What? What'd you say?" David said, skating up beside Mike.

"Oh nothing. I must have been thinking out loud," he kept his smile to himself.

Mike's thoughts turned to Angela and his paranoia. The last thing he wanted was to make both of them mad at him; they were his best friends. What if he and Angela got into a fight? He really liked her but was mired by his insecurities. How would his friendship with David be affected? It was a conundrum.

The lighted street up ahead snapped Mike out of his skate-induced trance. Cedric reached it first and let out a big whoop.

"Yeah buddy! This is Alameda Street boys. We'll ride it until we get to Copia," he called excitedly.

Cedric gave his board several strong, quick pushes and took the lead again. Up ahead, the lights at the Piedras Street bridge changed. A couple of cars rolled up and over. They were a little less than a mile away from the first big milestone – the intersection of Piedras and Alameda. The next landmark would be Copia and Alameda, another mile and a half up the road. From there, they'd be home in less than ten minutes.

"Not bad." Mike thought, "We really made good time. We'll be home soon."

The boys pushed their boards faster. Alameda Street was smooth as glass and felt good under their boards. Mike had heard someone say that skateboarding on a smooth street felt like sliding on a melting stick of butter. He had never realized what the guy meant until this moment. He was in pure skateboard nirvana.

A slight breeze and the dark night cooled the friends as they rolled onward. Even though Mike was feeling guilty, he was thoroughly enjoying the skate home.

The lights at the Piedras Street bridge loomed closer with every push of his board. Unnoticed, Cedric and David had picked up their pace, leaving Mike a block behind.

"Yo dudes, wait up!" Mike called after them but they were too far ahead to hear.

He started pushing faster, but David and Cedric kept up their pace. He fell further behind with every push. He'd never seen David skate so fast.

Mike was a little more than a block away from the bridge when his friends reached the intersection. They each had their boards in hand - ready to run across the street as the light changed or they got their chance, whichever came first.

He spotted a car speeding and weaving down the bridge toward the intersection. He became increasingly worried as the drunk driver continued. His parents' deaths flashed in his mind as his breathing sped. The memory and the sight before him chilled him to his bones.

Suddenly the car bounced over the median and swerved head on into the path of an approaching car. A loud explosion pierced the night as the cars met. Crunching metal, breaking glass and human screams combined into one terrifyingly loud noise, each part indistinguishable from the other.

The impact sent the vehicles careening away from each other. The drunk driver's car veered toward the teenagers. The other rolled into a storefront in the opposite direction. It hit the bricks and burst into flames.

Mike was stunned. It was the single scariest moment of his life. He shook his head trying to make sense of the scene unfolding before him. Everything was moving in slow motion.

He watched helplessly as the drunk's Mercedes raced toward his friends. They didn't move, frozen in their tracks. Mike screamed at them but couldn't hear his own words. Just as the hurtling car reached them, he heard a loud thud. Both boys flew to the side, Cedric tumbling headfirst over David's rolling body. A skateboard spun end over end through the night air. The sedan continued, running into a utility pole and coming to a dead stop.

The teenagers lay still, face down on the ground. Mike ran to them, tears welling in his eyes, anguish shrieking inside. He was a half a block away when they started moving.

"David! Cedric! Are you guys all right?" he yelled as he ran up, board in hand.

David cautiously sat up, inspecting his wounds. "Looks like I'm just a little scraped up."

"Me too, just minor stuff," Cedric added.

"Can you feel everything?" Mike questioned eyeing his friends, not believing they had made it through the accident unscathed.

Cedric stood, carefully shaking his arms then legs. "Yeah. I'm OK."

"Me too," David concurred.

"I thought you were dead... It looked bad."

"No. It didn't hit us, just my board," Cedric reassured his friend.

"Is everyone else alive?" David asked.

"I don't know," Mike said suddenly realizing there were still more victims. He looked around, focusing and pointing at the burning Lincoln Continental. "Let's get these people out first," he instructed as he ran toward the flames, friends in tow.

Gas had spilled and was burning near the tank. It was only a matter of time before the car blew. The unconscious driver was alone. Mike tried to open the driver's door but it was locked. David ran to the passenger side, gaining entry and reaching over to open it. Mike pulled the man out of the vehicle, dragging him a safe distance away from the fire.

The clean cut, sharply dressed man was breathing shallowly. There was a large, bloody bruise where his forehead impacted the steering wheel. Despite his injuries, he was coming to. Right then a car pulled up. The driver got out and ran over to them.

"What happened?" he asked. "Are you boys all right?"

"We pulled him out of the burning car. He was knocked out but is starting to come around," Mike replied. "If you can stay here, we'll check on the other car."

"Sure thing," said the good Samaritan. "I'll call 911."

The boys ran to the offending car. The driver was still in his seat, his body slumped forward, moaning and swinging his head from side to side. His door had opened and folded outward from the force of the wreck.

Mike was suddenly consumed with a burning rage - the man was obviously drunk. How could he endanger other people? Mike momentarily hesitated, disgusted and unsure he wanted to help. Despite his feelings, he continued the rescue.

He reached across and unclipped the seatbelt, putting the man's left arm around his shoulders and lifting him out. The man moaned in pain as Mike carried him to a clearing nearby.

The sounds of sirens wailed in the distance. They calmed Mike as he and David watched over the injured, drunk driver. Meanwhile, Cedric went back to the other victim.

At that moment, the drunk's mouth began foaming. He fell over and started to convulse. Instinctively, Mike laid him down, trying to relax him. When the seizures stopped, the man lay there, staring blindly and shivering. Mike took off his shirt and placed it over him. He was standing shirtless as the first emergency vehicles began arriving on the scene.

The accident site became a blur of activity. Policemen secured the area, red and blue flashing lights announcing their arrival. The ambulances held back, waiting for directions. Emergency medical technicians jumped out and ran supplies to the injured parties.

Mike had never seen an accident like this. Despite the trauma, everyone maintained their composure. Like doctors performing triage on a battlefield, paramedics carefully but quickly cared for their charges, the still burning flames illuminating their coordinated efforts.

Before long, the injured were packed into the ambulances and on their way to local hospitals. Wreckers were on the scene. The Mercedes was so totaled it had to be loaded on a flatbed. The Lincoln's charred remains lay lifelessly, toe-tagged, waiting to be transferred to the morgue.

The boys were beat. It was 3:30 a.m. and they were still far from home. As the last ambulance rolled out, a group of three police officers looked over at the forlorn friends. One of them walked in their direction. The other two hopped into their cruiser and sped off.

"Hi boys," said the tall, mustachioed cop. "I'm Officer Hernandez, "I hear you witnessed the whole disaster and helped save some lives."

"Yes sir," Mike said, in a weary voice.

"How about you boys, did you see anything?"

"I heard a loud noise and by the time I turned to look, the car was about to hit us," David offered. "If Cedric hadn't grabbed me and jumped, I think I would've been killed. It was coming right at us."

"I also heard it. I saw the car coming straight at us. At first I couldn't move, but finally did the only thing I could. It was awful."

The tall cop took notes as the boys spoke, occasionally looking up and nodding his head or redirecting with another question. As Cedric finished recanting his version, the cop looked around, shaking his head.

"Did any of you see bottles or cans of alcohol in either car?"

"No, but the driver who caused the accident was drunk," Mike insisted. "You should have seen him weaving across the bridge. I'm surprised he didn't fly off the side. He looked plastered."

"Did you smell alcohol on his breath?"

Mike tensed. He hadn't smelled alcohol when he was pulling the man out. In fact, he clearly remembered smelling something like sulfur. It reminded him of the smell Asarco emitted in its prime, its tall, dirty smokestacks pumping out thick clouds of black smoke.

"No officer. I didn't smell alcohol, but I smelled sulfur or something."

"Yeah," Officer Hernandez replied. "We didn't smell alcohol either. And sulfur's not something you'd smell on a person who's been drinking."

"So you think he wasn't drunk?"

"I didn't say that, but it's more likely to be something else, or even a combination of factors. It's hard to say until the investigation's finished."

"Isn't there an alcohol that you can't smell, you know, like vodka or gin?" Mike was persistent, not wanting to dismiss it so readily.

"That's what some people think, but alcohol smells like alcohol no matter what. It's hard to disguise."

Officer Hernandez gently patted Mike on the shoulder, "Don't worry. We'll find out what it is, and if he's guilty of driving under the influence of something, we'll nail him for it. I promise you."

Changing the subject, he half-jokingly asked Mike, "How'd you get those scabs and bruises, a fight?"

Mike smiled immediately and glanced at his smirking friends. He chuckled, "The only fight I've been in was with my skateboard. I fell doing a 50/50 on a handrail."

"What's a 50/50?" the officer looked truly interested.

"That's where you ollie onto a handrail, land on your trucks and grind down it." Mike spoke more enthusiastically as he explained.

"What's an ollie?"

"It's a jump without using your hands. You pop the tail of the board and jump at the same time. Like this." Mike set down his skateboard and eagerly popped a knee-high ollie.

"Wow! I've seen kids practicing those in parking lots."

"So I ollied onto the handrail and grinded down super fast." He used his hands to demonstrate. "When I landed, I kept moving but my board stopped." Mike slammed his fist into his hand. "I fell on this side." Mike proudly displayed his body-long trail of scabs and bruises.

"You need to be careful son. You only have one body, you know."

The friends smiled knowingly, having each heard that from other adults. They had always healed from their injuries, their bravado still intact – something the grown-ups had lost long ago.

"It's like this," Cedric pitched in, "There's a certain rush you get from putting it all on the line. When you skate, you put it all out there. Injuries are just part of it. The key is to minimize the damage. That's what separates the men from the boys."

"I had a skateboard with clay wheels when I lived in Florida, but that was only for a few hours," Officer Hernandez said. "I picked it up at a school near my house. Took it home and painted it a hideous shade of brown. While waiting for it to dry, my dad and brothers and this kid come into the garage. Turns out, the skateboard belonged to the kid. They had all been in the park playing football and saw me take it. Well this kid gets mad and starts crying cause now his board is painted an ugly brown color. Man did I get in trouble that day."

The friends shared a good laugh. "Clay wheels, what a Flintstone!" Cedric chided.

"Getting back to the accident, I've got another question. Who pulled the injured drivers out of their cars?"

"Mike and David," Cedric said.

"Actually, Mike pulled the drunk driver out of his car alone. He got to him before I could."

Cedric added, "If it wasn't for Mike, we might be dead. I heard you yelling at us after the cars wrecked. If it wasn't for that, I don't think I would have reacted soon enough. We owe you."

Mike was speechless. After all, he merely reacted to the situation at hand. He knew they would've done the same.

"Mike's the true hero," David proclaimed. "You'll never meet a better man. You should have seen him working on that drunk guy. He even gave him his t-shirt till the ambulance came."

"I'll make sure the gentlemen know who their saviors are. You boys deserve some recognition for your efforts. The world could use more good Samaritans like you. Without your help, both of those men could have died. You are brave men. All of you. Heroes."

His words touched them. Helping a fellow man came to them naturally, an unstated creed.

"There's a call coming through. Wait here." Officer Hernandez walked briskly to his car and reached for the microphone. When he turned toward the boys, his face looked concerned and agitated. That's when they heard the words clearly. "Officer down."

The cop jumped into his squad car and started the engine. He shifted into drive and pulled a squealing U-turn toward the boys.

"Sorry guys," he yelled from the car, "I wanted to give you a ride home, but duty calls. It's past curfew, so you all get home. If you get stopped by other police officers, have them call me. Stay safe – danger's everywhere."

With that, he sped off, tires screeching loudly, leaving a trail of smoke behind them.

The boys were alone with their boards once again. The street was littered with broken glass, metal, and puddles of gas and oil. An eerie feeling sent shivers down Mike's spine.

It was almost 4 a.m.

Chapter

9

The boys stood on the street corner for what seemed an eternity, drenched in the realism of their fate and close call with death. They were lucky to be alive, injury free. They felt different, older - like men.

Mike broke the heavy silence, "Well, looks like we still have a way to go. You guys want to get started or what?" He turned to his friends, who were oblivious to his inquiry - their minds lay elsewhere, between here and there.

"Can you believe what just happened?" Cedric asked emphatically. "Do... you... realize what happened?" He grabbed David's shoulders and shook them gently.

Mike and David were startled by their friend's intensity. David glanced at Mike for his reaction. Mike raised his eyebrows, then looked back at Cedric.

Cedric waved his hand in a sweeping motion. "We almost got killed here David. The car was so close it hit my board."

"Look. It bruised my knuckles. Do you realize how close we came to death? We almost got killed tonight, dude."

Cedric started sobbing quietly and hung his head to hide the tears, his body shuddered slightly as he let out a deep sigh. David moved a little closer and put his arm around his friend's shoulder.

"You never know... David. You never know when it's your turn. I've never thought about dying. I'm gonna feel blessed the rest of my life." He turned his head away and held a finger to one nostril, blowing it clean and doing the same to the other.

"Thanks for pushing me out of the way buddy. I owe you big time." David proclaimed. "I would never have saved myself. I'll never forget that Cedric. Never."

It was an emotional event, tears were flowing. The boys were drained. Mike's eyes remained perfectly dry. Experience had taught him to focus on what was, not what could've been. He was deeply moved and grateful his two best friends had escaped with their lives.

"We better start heading home guys," Mike suggested. "I'm sure my grandmother's ready to send out a search party for me. If we see a pay phone, I need to stop and give her a call. If we're lucky, maybe Uncle Ralph will be home and sober enough to pick us up."

They got on their boards and pushed away from ground zero. The damaged store's proprietor was now at the scene. He was talking loudly on his cell phone about the destruction, yelling that he couldn't just leave the store alone without a front window, he needed someone out there right now, and he didn't care how much it cost, his insurance would cover it.

He glared at the boys as they passed, ignorant of the night's young heroes, concluding they were looters. His disdainful glare reflected years of dealing with break-ins and burglaries.

Like the battle ruins in Mad Max, thin, wispy trails of smoke hung low in the air. An acrid odor stung their nostrils, a mixture of gas, burning rubber and melting asphalt. The boys pushed on.

Signs of the mayhem littered the street - nuts, bolts, broken pieces of glass and lots of unidentifiable parts. Beyond the wreckage, all was normal. Two worlds lived side by side, one destroyed, one leading to the safety of their homes.

"Where to now Ced?" asked David.

"Let's stay on Alameda to Raynolds. Once we cross over I-10 we're practically home. It's only another 2 miles or so."

"Remember, if we see a phone, I need to give my grandmother a call." Mike reminded the troupe as they pushed onward.

Thump, thump, thump, thump, thump. An annoyed Cedric quickly realized his wheel had a flat spot. Turning a deaf ear to it, he pressed on. All Cedric felt was flat spot, flat spot, flat spot.

Mike spied a pay phone in the middle of the block, between a beat up motel and an automotive repair shop. It was dark. Businesses were closed and the streets abandoned. A weak neon light buzzed and announced the Drop Inn Motel.

Mike picked up the receiver but heard no dial tone. He dropped two quarters in, but they fell through and popped out of the change slot onto the sidewalk. One quarter rolled toward the rain gutter. Mike stomped on it and picked it up. He tried a second time, but they fell straight through again. This time into his waiting hand.

"Maaaaaaan, this phone is broken," Mike moaned. "Where are the skateboard gods when you need them?" he asked half jokingly.

"I'm not surprised," Cedric remarked. "My tio says junkies rip them off to pay for drugs. He knew a guy from high school who would make a couple of hundred bucks a night vandalizing phones."

"So why do they keep putting them in?" David asked.

"Because a lot of the poor people around here can't afford their own. It would be discrimination if they only put phones in the good parts of town." Cedric replied.

"Let's keep going. There'll be another phone up ahead," Mike said.

"I don't think so, eh-se."

Every head turned toward the dark figure emerging from the shadows. An ominous man in his early twenties with a ponytail and goatee slouched and stared at them menacingly. He sported gang tattoos on his face and arms, a white wife beater t-shirt and khaki chinos. His pointed black dress shoes shined from the recent polishing and his blue bandana hung low over his eyes.

"Give me jur skateboards now. We should have taken them earlier." He pulled a long black item from his pocket. The boys heard a click and saw a flash of silver. The hood stepped forward, a six-inch switchblade held up for effect.

"Come on man. We need our skateboards to get home," David pleaded with the attacker. "We don't want any trouble. Can't you just let us skate off?"

"Why would I want to do that? Give me jur skateboards now before I cut jou!"

He lunged at the boys. Instinctively, Cedric swung his board hard at the gangster. It connected with the hood's skull, making a loud cracking sound. He collapsed to the ground, out cold.

"Come on," Cedric called as he hopped on his board, pushing down the street as fast as he could. "We've got to get out of here. These guys don't play around. Hurry!"

Mike and David were on his tail skating at speeds they usually reserved for daylight hours. They skated so fast, they were three blocks away before the hood revived.

Fear propelled them. Not a word had been spoken since starting their get-away. They kept pushing toward safety, wanting nothing more than to be in their homes. They were still more than two miles away.

Like a scene from Outer Limits, the streets were void of human life. Occasionally, a lone car passed or a sleeping drunk in a doorway stirred. The filth, decay and poverty reeked of a third world favela. It stood in stark contrast to the clean neighborhoods only a couple of miles away.

They skated past little Mom and Pop grocery stores, liquor stores, meat markets, icehouses, and plumbing supply stores. They also passed about every type of automobile repair shop imaginable: radiators, air conditioning, tires, tune-ups, painting, dent removal, upholstery. Occasionally, dogs ran up to their fences, barking at the boys, warning them not to enter their domain.

Suddenly, a loud, screeching noise stopped the boys in their tracks. They looked back and saw a car barreling toward them. They scooped up their boards and jumped on the sidewalk. The car hauled to a stop and the doors all flew open.

"Uh oh," David exclaimed, "This doesn't look good. Get ready guys."

The first one out of the car was the guy Cedric had just knocked out cold. The swelling and truck marks on his face gave him a monster-like quality His soulless eyes focused on the boy who had defiled him.

The remaining hoods were equally threatening. The largest stood well over six feet and proudly displayed his prison tattoos on his neck and around his eyes. His bulging biceps highlighted more chilling gang symbols. The others, though smaller, were extremely pissed off and were ready to throw down with the skaters.

The mangled assailant stood face to face with Cedric. The other three held back. Mike and David kept their distance also, boards held ready for action.

"Hey eh-se, why'd jou hit me with jur skateboard? I should keel jou right here and now mang."

"You were trying to steal our skateboards. We told you we needed them and you tried to attack us. It was only self-defense man," Cedric appealed.

"Tell that to the judge fool. I don't care. Jou mess with me eh-se, jou mess with the Homeless Gang." His three cohorts boldly flashed their gang signs.

Cedric remained quiet. He never took his eyes off the proclaimed gangster. After a short silence, the thug threw his hands up, narrowly missing the sides of Cedric's head.

"What, never heard of us? Jou gots to be kidding."

"Of course we've heard of you guys," Cedric mustered, "I wasn't looking for trouble with you. I was only trying to protect us."

"By knocking me out eh-se? I'm gonna cut jou man." Once again he pulled out his switchblade and flicked it open. "Prepare to die." He kept one eye on Cedric and the other on his board as he spoke.

His crew stood up straighter at this announcement, brandishing their weapons. The ex-con wielded a switchblade, while the other two pulled out guns. One pointed at Mike, the other at David.

Mike was ready to fight but knew the guns stacked the odds. He steeled his mind and grabbed his board tighter, ready to swing at the first unwelcome advance.

He looked at his friends. Cedric was still face to face with his aggressor. David stood at the ready, just like Mike.

Suddenly, Mike heard two loud bangs. Before he could determine who had been shot, thick red smoke filled the air. It was impossible to see more than a couple of inches in any direction.

"Don't anyone move! Put your weapons down, now! Slide them toward the sound of my voice. If anyone does anything funny, I'll cut you down with my M-16. If you want to take a chance, come on out and meet some hot lead."

Mike couldn't believe his ears. In the midst of all the chaos, once again, the sounds of safety - Uncle Ralph. Almost immediately, he heard guns and knives sliding along the sidewalk, then silence.

"OK now. Skaters, walk to me. Punks run the other way if you know what's good for you. Be gone before the smoke disappears. If I see you, I'll blow your ass away. DO IT NOW!" He shouted the last command.

The hoods ran in the opposite direction. Mike walked toward his uncle's voice, making out the shapes of David and Cedric as he neared the edge of the red smoke. Uncle Ralph stood - M-16 in one hand, smoke grenade in the other. He looked like a mad man. This was the Ralph Mike had only heard about.

The hoods' car, a lowrider Cadillac painted light blue with rose vines as accent stripes, was still parked on the street - motor running. Everything on the inside of the Caddy was pretty much white, from the dice on the rearview mirror to the fuzzy upholstery on the seats. It was blinding.

Ralph leaned the knives against the curb. With one forceful stomp he broke both blades. He grabbed the guns and shoved them in his waistband. Walking over to the lowrider, he pulled a metal object out of his pocket and tapped the front windshield, shattering the glass. He repeated the taps until every window was broken. Methodically, he turned his attention to the tires, removing all four valves, incapacitating the vehicle. Lastly, he yanked the keys from the ignition and hurled them over a building across the street, saying to himself, "This'll keep them from following us."

Turning toward his car, he motioned the boys to get in. He pulled the pin on his last smoke grenade, and in one last act of defiance, tossed it through the broken windshield. Smoke instantly filled the lowrider.

Uncle Ralph coolly got behind the wheel and steered homeward. Mike looked admiringly at his uncle and smiled. He had never seen him in action. Tonight he was a superhero.

"That was the most amazing thing ever. Thanks." David cautiously patted Ralph's shoulder as he spoke.

"Not nearly as amazing as some of the recon I had to do over in Iraq, son. Now, that was some real scary stuff. El Paso hoodlums are nothing. They have it too soft."

"How did you know where we were?"

"You were easy to find! You left a trail of breadcrumbs. Luckily, I always carry smoke bombs in case I need flares. I just got a laser scope on my M-16 last week and it was still in my car. Good thing I didn't have to use it 'cause I don't have ammo. We got lucky."

The boys laughed and relaxed a little. It had been a long night. One that started with fun and skating and ended with Ralph saving their lives - an epic night that had changed their destinies.

Uncle Ralph pulled up to Cedric's, a very pretty little two-bedroom house, neatly manicured. There were half a dozen cars parked in front, suggesting many occupants lived inside - a common arrangement in this part of town.

David grabbed Cedric's arm as he exited the car. "I owe you one bro. You saved my life more than once tonight." Tears involuntarily welled in David's eyes. He had never carried a debt like this.

Cedric bumped fists with David. "Tonight was a blast, we've got to do it again sometime," he mocked with a twisted smile and wrinkled forehead. All three boys shared a nervous laugh.

"I guess we won't be skating the Worm today?" Cedric snickered.

"I think Mike needs his beauty sleep. He's got a big night planned with Angela. We can skate the Worm next week."

"Oooo, Angela," Cedric said. "Sounds good to me. I'm dog tired."

"You better get inside now Cedric. I'm sure your family's worried about you," Uncle Ralph interrupted.

"Thanks again Uncle Rambo, I mean Ralph," Cedric joked. "You're a life saver. Thanks for getting us out of that jam with the Toothless hoods. That was classic. I'll tell that story to my grandchildren someday."

"And the entire school on Monday," David laughed. "This story's too good to keep to ourselves!"

"Get out while you're ahead kid," Uncle Ralph chuckled. "Get out while you're ahead."

Mike kept an eye on his friend as they pulled away. Cedric's mom hugged her son, pulling him in and closing the door behind her. The porch light turned off and Mike returned to his reflections.

Mike felt secure knowing he was with those he loved and trusted. It had been a long night with many lessons. He now looked forward to the comfort of his waiting bed and the promise of a long, deep slumber.

They pulled up to David's dark, silent house. Mrs. Davis slept soundly inside. Her earplugs had ensured her oblivion to the night's events. She hadn't heard the police calls earlier, just as she now didn't hear Uncle Ralph's car pulling up with her son

Uncle Ralph studied the boys. Both were disheveled and looked beat. Ralph wanted to impart fatherly words of wisdom that would hopefully cement the meaning of the night in their consciousness. He began slowly.

"Well boys, you're both safe and the night's over. Hope you learned some lessons tonight. As you get older, you'll look back on this and draw from it. Try to learn from your mistakes. Otherwise, valuable lessons will slip away."

"You're right Uncle Ralph. I learned a lot tonight," David replied. "If it wasn't for you, Mike and Cedric, I'd be dead." His gaze focused on Mike while he spoke.

Ralph reflected on the friends he lost in the Gulf War, offering, "Friends are a valuable commodity to have in this world."

"I learned that just because a taco comes from a place called Dog Tacos, it doesn't mean they are made from dogs," Mike chuckled, trying to lighten the mood.

"It's good to see you learned something tonight," Uncle Ralph said, raising his eyebrows and laughing at Mike's fixation. "Yeah. I had a taste of dog in the Gulf once. It was actually pretty good."

Mike and David exchanged grossed-out looks and feigned vomiting, which led Mike into an actual fit of dry-heaves.

"I seriously doubt they're better than Chico's," Uncle Ralph proclaimed ignoring the boys' sideshow.

"You'll see. I'll always be a loyal Chico's fan but Dog Tacos rules... and their salsa..." Mike salivated, his voice trailing off.

"They sound good, but right now David needs to get to bed."

"Yeah. I'll see you all tomorrow. What time should Angela be ready?"

Uncle Ralph shot Mike a glance out of the corner of his eye, smiled broadly and gave him a jab in the arm.

"Tell her I'll pick her up at six."

"Where are you taking her?" David asked.

"I don't know," Mike replied. "Maybe we'll go out for some Dog Tacos," he winked.

"Remember, you're an American citizen, and buses stop running at midnight, OK?"

"Yep, I'm American and the bus turns into a pumpkin at midnight. Got it."

Mike and David laughed, bumping each other's fists before David got out of the car. The tail of his board made a shushing sound as he dragged it along the sidewalk. He was ragged and worn out, walking much slower than usual.

"Home Jeeves," Mike commanded his driver.

"Don't push your luck, punk," Uncle Ralph grumbled. "Do you know how worried your grandmother's been? You really caused her a lot of grief today. You're not going to do that again, are you? If Mom says you can go on your date, OK. Sunday you'll be in the yard working. Got it?"

Mike smiled. Uncle Ralph was coming down hard on him, but it felt good to know he cared.

Mike counted his blessings before saying, "Anything Uncle Ralph. I can start as early as seven if you want."

Uncle Ralph grinned. Mike was such a good kid. He had never caused any real trouble. "Not bad for a teenager," he mused.

"Seven's too early little bro. We'll get started at nine and work till about four." Ralph continued, "Don't plan anything - you'll be grounded all day Sunday. Comprende?"

"Sure do Unk."

"Sounds like a hell of a night. Tonight's mission is top secret. Don't tell mom about the hoods, guns and smoke grenades. Okay?" He smiled proudly. This had been his biggest thrill since the war.

"Sure," Mike agreed. "Hey, are you going to give me a smoke grenade or an M-16 when I get a car?"

Uncle Ralph laughed. "We'll see tough guy."

Mike heaved a sigh of relief. Telling Grandmother about the knives and guns was the last thing he wanted to do.

They pulled into the driveway of their small home. Even by modest standards, it was tiny. Its two small bedrooms, one bathroom, tiny kitchen, nearly nonexistent living room and Ralph's bedroom converted from the one-car garage, kept the family sheltered.

Mike slowly got out of the car, pulling his skateboard out as he rose. Wisps of red rode the mostly gray skies. Dawn was still another twenty minutes away.

Mike braced himself, anticipating his grandmother's reaction.

Chapter

10

Mike was halfway to the door when it swung open. It was almost 6 a.m. There stood his grandmother in her robe, curlers in her hair and dark circles under her eyes. A big smile spread across her face as she motioned for him to come inside.

"Mikey," she squealed, pinching his cheeks and pulling him in for a tight hug. "I've been so worried. It sounds like you had quite a night. The news stations are calling you heroes. You should be proud of yourselves."

"The news," Mike repeated. "It was too late for the news."

"After I spoke to the customs officer, I turned on the television. They interrupted the show with a special report. They said two drivers had been injured in a terrible accident."

"It was horrible. David and Cedric almost got run over by the drunk guy." Mike said excitedly. "They were almost splattered."

"They mentioned some late-night skateboarders were almost hit. That's when they said your name and explained how you helped," Mike's grandmother continued. "They didn't say anything about a drunk driver. I think the driver who caused the accident was in diabetic shock."

"I'm pretty sure he was drunk!"

"That's not what they said."

Mike was stunned. He had condemned the man as a worthless drunk, no different than the one who had killed his parents. He had misjudged the man. Suddenly, he felt very small - not at all like a hero. He felt a little ill.

Yesterday, Mrs. Johnson expressed concern over his anger. Maybe he really was repressing his emotions. Maybe he did need counseling. He decided to make a serious effort when he met with Beverly.

"You need to get to bed," Uncle Ralph interrupted his nephew's resolve. "You have a date tonight."

"What do you mean a date?" Grandmother asked with a twinkle in her eye.

"Yeah Mom, it seems our little Miguel is going out with Angela tonight. What do you think about that?"

"Is that right Mikey?"

"Yes ma'am, it is."

"Where are you going?"

"We'll probably go to a movie, maybe get a bite to eat afterward. Nothing much really."

"My Mikey, going on his first date," she gushed. "Are you excited? I bet Angela is."

Mike made a strained look and replied. "More like nervous. What if Angela has a lousy time? You know, I don't have much money. I don't want her to think I'm cheap."

"Don't worry about Angela. She's had a crush on you for years. The main thing you need to realize is that Angela's going on the date because she likes being with you. Relax, it's going to be fun."

"Yeah, Angela says she likes me, but…"

"Don't be nervous. Get some sleep, the date will be perfect." She patted his cheek and turned him toward the bedroom. "Get to bed. You need your rest." Her eyes beamed brightly.

Mike couldn't get in bed fast enough. He fell asleep as his head hit the pillow. His clothes lay crumpled in a heap at the foot of the bed. His skateboard had landed on his school backpack, wheels up. One shoe lay upside down next to the bed; the other hung precariously from his foot, his body askew and face down.

He dreamed heavily as he slept. His mind replayed the night's events. Angela, the Homeless Gang, Dog Tacos, the incident at the border, the accident, and the incident involving Uncle Ralph. So many extraordinary things had happened in one short night. Mike's racing mind did not afford him much rest.

When he woke up, it was four o'clock. Mike had slept almost nine hours. Even so, he felt drained and mentally exhausted. Last night's many near death experiences weighed heavily on his soul. He was emotionally spent.

Beat, he got out of bed and made his way to the bathroom. His cuts faintly summoned him, no longer screaming of their pain. Flakes of hardened blood and skin hung loosely on to the outer edges of his wounds. The healing process was well under way.

For the first time Mike noticed how quickly he was recovering. He decided next time he'd actually clean and bandage the cuts before going to bed. It would help speed the process. In a parallel thought, Mike realized he could also speed his emotional healing by meeting with Beverly Diaz and participating fully. Suddenly, the thought of counseling thrilled him.

His bruises were no longer dark purple and red, a good sign. They were turning brown and yellow, as if his flesh were rotting from the inside out. This didn't bother Mike - a healing bruise was never pretty.

He went to the sink, splashed some water on his face, and set the timer for five minutes before starting the shower. Almost immediately, Mike could feel the heat of the steam rising. He jumped in. Like the gun battles in Uncle Ralph's stories, a million tiny hot pellets sprayed across him.

He aimed the spray at his cuts and bruises to loosen them. They didn't sting nearly as bad as yesterday, another good sign. The water soothed his sore body immediately. Hanging his head under the shower spray, Mike lost himself in thought.

What would he wear tonight? Should he wear his sneakers or dress shoes? What will he talk about with Angela? What about David? Uggh... Suddenly, Mike's stomach tightened and began to ache. He had butterflies. He'd had them before but usually before sporting events, like when he was eleven years old and at his first karate match.

He had worked hard all year. As he stood in the arena, his stomach ached and he felt a little out of breath. Across from Mike was his opponent, twice his size and twenty times meaner.

The battle began. Mike was small but agile and fast. His coach had done his job well. Mike understood he could not rely on his size. Instead, he had to use his knowledge, skill and speed. On the contrary, his large, muscular opponent was counting on his brute size and strength.

When it was over, Mike had won his first karate match, but he was never able to conquer the butterflies. They showed up at every one of his matches. He never got butterflies fighting opponents at the dojo in practice. They only seemed to appear in competition.

Now, thinking about his upcoming date with Angela, the butterflies made an appearance again. Although this time, it was a little different than before. There was no large, hulking opponent. There was just sweet, innocent Angela.

Though Mike felt confident tonight's date would go well, he was unsure and nervous about the impact it might have. Could he and David still be best friends? Would Mrs. Davis still like him if they broke up? The most important question of all was would Angela want to see him again?

"I'm sailing in uncharted waters," he said to himself. "Hope I don't capsize tonight." He hadn't planned on using two nautical clichés in one sentence and laughed at how corny they sounded. He was two-and-a-half minutes into his shower, two-and-a-half minutes to go.

Where would he take Angela? Something else to stress about. Would he be able to come up with a date they could both enjoy? So far his best idea was going to a movie at the mall and then eating at one of the many eateries in the Food Court or Chico's, but that's what all of the high school kids did and he wanted this to be different. He wasn't quite sure how to make it special on his limited budget.

His mind wandered to Angela's beauty and her disarming bright smile. Occasionally, Mike would find himself staring at her, tuning out her words. She'd ask if anything was wrong. The best he could muster was, "Just thinking about a tough homework assignment," or "A small problem at home, nothing to worry about."

He found it increasingly difficult to repress his true feelings for her. The more she expressed hers, the harder it was to deny his own. His resolve was suddenly cemented. He was going to date Angela. Whatever happened would happen. "BUZZZZZZ!" The timer sounded, abruptly ending his shower and ponderings.

He brushed his teeth and combed his hair, putting on his nicest boxers, "Lucky Charms" - so named because they were covered with little green clovers. This would prove to be the only easy decision in selecting the night's wardrobe.

Most of his clothes were skateboard- or school-related. His heart sunk as he searched for something appropriate. After several agonizing searches, he settled on a pair of rarely worn jeans that were too new, crisp and tight. He put on a dark blue button-up shirt he'd never worn over a fairly new charcoal colored Reptile Skateboards t-shirt. He completed the look with a dark pair of socks to match his only non-skateboard shoes, brown Wayfarers.

He sat on the corner of his unmade bed, picked up the remote control, and turned on the television and Nintendo. Almost instantly, he became engrossed in the new Tony Hawk game he had picked up the week before. He was deep into a double kick flip to fakie nose grind when he heard a knock at the front door.

His grandmother answered the door but everything sounded muffled. He strained to hear – not recognizing the other voice. A moment later, footsteps in the hall were followed by a knock on his door.

"Mike there is someone who wants to speak to you in the living room. Could you come out please?"

"OK, Grandma. Let me finish getting dressed and I'll be right out."

Mike took one last look in the mirror. He tousled his hair with his fingers, making sure he had the right effect. As he walked into the living room, Mike was surprised by the sizeable man sitting on the couch. He looked vaguely familiar. Maybe he had seen him down at the Social Security offices.

His grandmother sat facing the couch, both had glasses of iced tea in front of them. A large glass pitcher sat in the middle of the coffee table with sliced lemons floating on the surface. Her lemon tea was Mike's favorite beverage. He swore it had revived him many a time after a heated skate session. She looked up as he entered. Immediately, the stranger stood up and extended his large hand toward Mike.

He stood about six feet tall and appeared to be in good shape for a man his age. His hair was silvery white, smoothed back and made shiny by the copious amounts of expensive, coconut pomade. He was impeccable. He wore an expensive, silky grey suit with thin, finely woven pinstripes and sharp, grey leather lace up shoes with wingtips. His perfectly ironed, crisp white shirt accented the outfit regally. He had a platinum ring with a large, sparkling diamond on his right hand, and a gold Rolex watch adorned his left. He looked like a million bucks, if you looked past the mess on his face.

"Maybe this is one of Uncle Ralph's latest victims," Mike continued thinking, trying to figure out how he knew the stranger who was shaking his hand like he was quick playing a slot machine. "Can't be. He wouldn't be so well-dressed and nice to me if Uncle Ralph had just beat him up."

"Hi Mike. I'm Walter McCoy. I was one of the people you helped last night in the car accident. Actually, I was the one who caused it. Officer Hernandez told me you pulled me out of my car and carried me to safety. I wanted to thank you personally." He had a slight Texas drawl and looked Mike directly in the eye when he spoke. Mike was taken aback by his bright, aquamarine eyes. Their intensity was captivating.

"That's right! I remember you. You were the drunk guy. I'm sorry, I didn't mean that."

"That's okay Mike. It was diabetic shock. I never touch alcohol... because of the diabetes. Although, I can understand why you may have thought I was drunk. I tell you, it's an inhumane disease. Wish I didn't have it. The hospital patched me up, gave me a shot, and sent me on my way this morning."

"I had taken a business trip and thought I had enough insulin with me. I took my last dose early yesterday. Usually I wouldn't have been driving, but my chauffeur was on vacation and I thought it would be all right. Boy did I figure wrong."

"I'm sorry. Is that why you smelled like sulfur?" Mike looked truly concerned as he spoke. He was coming to terms with his wrongful condemnation of Mr. McCoy. Unknowingly, he was also beginning to face his unresolved anger over the unjust and premature death of his parents.

Mr. McCoy's bright white, perfect, youthful teeth glistened as he sat back a little and said, "Please Mike, no need to be sorry. All I remember is a kind soul, risking his life to save mine. In fact, you helped save my life and the life of the person I hit. Not many people would have reacted as coolly as you and your friends did last night. If it weren't for you, I don't think I'd be sitting here today."

The grateful man shifted in his chair as he spoke, his long legs trying to get more comfortable. He choked back a lump in his throat and wiped a tear from the corner of his eye. It was strange to see such a large, strong man holding back tears like a skater who's just slammed but doesn't want to show his pain.

"And yes, I smelled like sulfur because of my toxic condition. Actually, I came here to see if I could help you in any way, Mike. You gave me back my life. I don't know how to repay what you have done. My life…" He blinked as he tried to regain his composure, but it looked more like a wince under the scratches, bruises and band-aids. "I've got to do something to repay your selflessness."

"Maybe you should talk to David and Cedric." Mike blurted out remembering how close Mr. McCoy had come to hitting them with his car. "You almost ran them over. Your car hit Cedric's skateboard and now he has a flat spot on his wheels. He's the one who could really use some help. Plus,

David and Cedric also helped take care of you and the other driver, not just me."

"You're a good friend Mike. I've already spoken to their families and we've worked out what I'll call my restitution. I'll make sure Cedric is compensated well for his skateboard."

"Mrs. Davis spoke highly of you. She cares very much for you. She also said you have a date with her daughter, Angela, tonight. Is that so?"

Mike turned a light shade of red as his face warmed with embarrassment. He still wasn't completely comfortable with the idea of dating his best friend's sister. Looking down at his hands, he muttered, "Yes, in fact I have to pick her up at six. I was getting ready when you came."

"Where are you going?"

"Well, I don't exactly know right now. I want this date to be special."

"Special?"

"You know, something other than a movie and dinner. The only problem is that's all I can think of."

"How about taking my limo?"

"Well, I was sort of hoping we'd be alone."

Mr. McCoy and Mike's grandmother shared a hearty laugh, remembering younger days and the anxious, tense moments of youth. Mike turned beet red. Hoping to leave Mike's ego intact, Mr. McCoy ceased his laughter and cleared his throat.

"Tell you what. I'll have Frank drop this old man off at home and come back for you. The limo's all yours," he chuckled.

"A limo?" Mike perked up. "I've never ridden in a limo!"

"How do you say it? That's how I roll?" Mr. McCoy winked. "Any time I'm not using it, it's yours - that's how you roll."

"You're kidding, right?" Mike asked bewildered. "This is how I roll?"

"Yes, Mike. You saved my life."

"I've heard that a lot lately."

"I don't follow."

"Well last night, if I hadn't yelled and Cedric hadn't pushed David he would've been run over. They said I saved their lives. Cedric was the real hero last night."

"Let me tell you what I've already told your friends. I am an old man. I have no family left. My only son was killed in a motorcycle accident ten years ago when he was sixteen. My wife divorced me shortly thereafter and died of cancer last year. I have no one else."

"I was blessed with a loving family for sixteen years. I will always be grateful for that. I've also been very successful and prosperous in business. Helping you get a good start would not only reward a deserving group but also bring much satisfaction and purpose to my life. I want very much to give you opportunities you wouldn't have had otherwise. What are your thoughts on college?"

"I'd love to go," Mike proudly replied. His grandmother smiled broadly. "I'm really hoping for a scholarship but the military is my back up. I've got really good grades, but you never know." He crossed his fingers for effect.

"Well son, my offer to you is this: Forget the military. Focus on your grades now so you'll get into the college of your choice. Don't worry about costs - I'll take care of that."

"Are you telling me you'll pay for any college?" Mike was incredulous. This had never been a part of his college plans.

"That's right," Mr. McCoy chuckled. "Any college you choose. Even UTEP if that's what you want. But a boy with your grades and my support should be thinking Ivy League. The world is your oyster Mike, or is that pearl? I never get that right."

Mike's grandmother cooed at the thought. "Just think Mikey, not only will you be our first college graduate, you might be an Ivy Leaguer at that." Love radiated from her eyes as she looked at Mike. "Mr. McCoy's your guardian angel. He's been sent to watch over you and help you on your next phase of life. Something I can't do."

"Now, I'm a proud woman and I don't believe in taking anyone's charity. You know that about me Mikey, right?"

"Yes ma'am." Mike looked at the coffee table, humbled by his grandmother's heartfelt words. Like the evening before, tonight was surreal.

"You did a good thing last night. You helped us without thinking of yourself. The good Lord sent you to me. He's now allowing an old man to find renewed meaning in his life. All I want is to help you with yours."

"I never want to see you leave El Paso Mijo, but this is an opportunity of a lifetime. You must take advantage of it and go to the best school you can. You deserve it baby." She choked on her last words.

Giving Mike up to the world was something she had been dreading for a long time. She had taken for granted Mike would go to UTEP. She had planned on having him for at least four more years. Now, in an instant and with a few words from a stranger, those four years disappeared.

Mike mumbled, "I feel like I'm supposed to say, 'Thank you, but no thank you'. You know, like they always do on TV."

"Mike, this isn't TV and I won't accept no for an answer. As long as your grandmother is OK with it, I'm here. Allow me that privilege, please." There was a slight look of desperation as he shifted nervously in his seat waiting for Mike's answer.

"If not for me, do it for your parents. I'm sure they would've wanted this for you. I know I wanted it for Rocky..." Tears welled in Mr. McCoy's eyes as he reflected on his long dead son and what never came to be.

"When Rocky had his motorcycle accident, he was out on Montana Street, past the city limits," Mr. McCoy spoke slowly, the utterance of his words incredibly painful. Until this moment, he had never spoken to anyone about that fateful night.

Choking on his words, Mr. McCoy continued. "The police said his front tire blew out and he careened off into the desert. When he didn't come home that night, we had crews looking for him for days. Some parolees cleaning the roadway spotted his bike and his lifeless body nearby. The coroner believes Rocky was still alive for a while. If someone had found him soon enough and helped him, like you and your friends did with me, he might still be here today. It wasn't in his destiny." The large man's tearful, piercing blue eyes were like glass.

Mike wanted to stop the pain but all he could do was stand there and hold back his own tears. Memories of his parents' untimely death throbbed in his head and heart, and his own agony melted with Mr. McCoy's.

"I owe it to Rocky to help you boys. Your friends have already accepted my offer, I hope you do too. What do you say?"

"Yes, Mr. McCoy. I'll take your offer, but you have to let me work off my tuition. I'll work for free."

"I don't want work to get in the way of your education. You need your study time. I'll tell you what. You can work for me summers if you let me pay you what I think you're worth. Do we have a deal on both the college and the work?" Mr. McCoy held his hand out to Mike.

Mike took the large hand with both of his and squeezed firmly. "Thank you, sir. You won't be sorry. You don't know how much this means to me. I'll be forever indebted."

"No son. It's me who will be forever indebted. Don't ever forget that. That must always be clear. Understand? It is you who saved my life: last night and again today by accepting my offer."

"Yes sir."

"And none of this sir stuff either. Please call me Walter. That's what my friends call me. Everyone else can call me Mr. McCoy." He smiled as he spoke.

"OK, Walter." Mike looked a little uncomfortable. He'd never called an adult by their first name.

"I have a friend who will help you apply to colleges. Her name is Maria Elenar. You choose the schools and I'll pay for your applications. OK?"

"Yes sir. I mean Walter."

"OK. Maria will call you this Monday and set up an appointment. Can't start this process too soon. Gotta get a jump on all the other applicants."

"Who is Maria?" Mike's grandmother asked.

"She's my right hand. She's a Harvard grad and sharp as a tack. She can have Mike's applications on the way to the schools before the week is out. You'll like her. She's intelligent, compassionate, and has a great sense of humor."

Walter stood up and nodded at Mike and his grandmother. "Right now I better get home. You don't want to be late for your date. It'll take Frank a half an hour to drop me off and get back, tops."

"Perfect timing," Mike grinned. "Angela's going to be really surprised when she sees your limousine. Thanks again for lending it to us."

"Think about all I've said Mike. I know it's a lot to digest in such a short time, but I truly want to have a positive hand in your life. Don't sell yourself short, ever."

"I won't, I promise. So, Mr. Frank will take us anywhere?"

"Anywhere you like."

Mike's eyes lit up. Finally, he knew what he could do for his date. "Even Juarez?"

"Sure. Even Juarez. What do you have in mind? Clubbing, dancing?"

"No, Dog Tacos."

"Dog Tacos?" Walter and Mike's grandmother exchanged confused glances. She shrugged her shoulders to make it clear she didn't know what Mike was talking about.

"It's really called El Taquito Mexicano. They make the best tacos anywhere! Except for yours, Grandma." Mike quickly clarified to protect his grandmother's feelings.

Walter laughed. "It's right off the main strip, right? Señor Lozano owns that place. He's a good friend of mine. I've eaten there many times. Best tacos around. He's going to get a kick out of your nickname. Dog Tacos! Ha! That's funny."

"I had them last night for the first time. I'd love to take Angela there."

"You got it Mike. I'll call my good buddy and make sure you're taken care of. In fact…"

Chapter

11

Mike couldn't believe his eyes. Through his bedroom window he spotted the long, shiny, new limo rounding the corner. Neighbors in their front yards watched as it pulled up in front of his house. Mrs. Bustamante, the watchful eye of the block, shaded her view as she tried her hardest to determine who was inside.

He took a last look in the mirror. Everything was in place and he looked good. He splashed on some Midnight Oil, a Christmas present Uncle Ralph had given him, teasing, "You never know when you may want to burn the midnight oil baby."

When the cologne hit his cuts, they burned sharply. "Ouch! Maybe that's what he meant," Mike chuckled to himself.

Hearing the doorbell buzz, he ran into the living room, yelling, "See you Grandma! I'm going now!"

"OK Sweetie," she called from the laundry room. "Make sure you have your wallet."

Grandmother always reminded him to check for his wallet when he left the house. His grandfather was almost deported to Mexico once because he couldn't prove he was an American citizen. Grandmother worried about all her kids after that.

Frank the chauffer was at the door, looking sharp and out of place in his freshly pressed black suit. Mrs. Bustamante crossed the street heading for Mike, never losing sight of Frank.

"Hi Mike. Nice limousine. Is it yours?" she asked facetiously.

"Hi, Mrs. Bustamante. No, it's not mine, but I'm using it tonight for a date."

"Wow. How'd you manage that?"

"A friend is lending it to me."

"A friend? Anyone I know?"

"No, Mrs. Bustamante, no one you know. It's a long story. I have to run or I'll be late," he hurriedly responded hoping to make a quick get-away.

Mrs. Bustamante was not easily dismissed. "Who are you taking out?"

"Angela Davis."

"Little Angie from up the street?"

"Yes ma 'am."

"Oh my goodness! I've watched the two of you grow up, playing together. I always knew you'd be more than friends someday. I can't believe the day has come."

"Seems like everyone knew this day was coming but me."

"That's the way it always is Mike. The man is always the last to know," Mrs. Bustamante laughed. She put her hands on her hips and shook her head. "Don't worry honey. You'll get used to it soon enough. Just remember, the woman's the one who's really in control. That's the way it is with me and Mr. Bustamante. That's just the way it is with most couples."

"OK, that's a scary thought but I'll try to remember that. I better get going." Mike didn't want to show up late and was anxious to leave. "I don't want to keep Angela waiting for our first date."

"And it's your first date," she said. "Hope you two have fun. Bye Mike." Mrs. Bustamante waved at him, feeling content with her newly acquired knowledge.

Mike had worked in Mrs. Bustamante's yard many times. He even mowed her grass for an entire summer. Not once had she offered him money. They lived on a tight budget, a small retirement and Social Security.

Mr. Bustamante was once the strongest man on the block. His industriousness and physical abilities were legendary in the neighborhood. He singlehandedly built the cement and rock fence around his property high enough to keep his Great Dane Harold from jumping over it. Not only was he solely responsible for the wall that still stood strong today but he had managed to do it after work and on the weekends over the sweltering months one summer in 105 degree heat.

He was also known to be one of the fastest and ablest workers at the local cement factory, earning him the title of shift foreman. His productivity was suddenly halted when he suffered a horrible accident loading a wheelbarrow full of heavy limestone rock into the cement barrel at work. In the blink of an eye, Mr. Bustamante was reduced to a shadow of his former self. He could no longer stand up straight. His doctors prohibited him from picking up anything weighing more than a gallon of milk. He was a proud man so shamed by his hunched over, paralyzed and painful slow walk that he usually opted to sit around watching television under the heavy effects of the opiates his doctor prescribed to manage his pain.

Mike liked to help around their house. In return, Mrs. Bustamante baked him large amounts of Mexican pastries. Sometimes he felt a little guilty because he purposely found things to do just so she'd make a batch of cookies or cream puffs. Her treats were irresistibly delicious; he would do the unthinkable for a bite.

He watched her disappear into her home and then turned to Frank who opened the door to the back seat of the black Lincoln Town Car. New car smell wafted from the rich brown Corinthian leather interior with finely crafted double-stitched seats and monogrammed emblems with "WM" finely sewn in calligraphy with golden thread. The expansive interior beckoned Mike to enter. He was blown away.

Frank pointed to a little refrigerator with a real wood door and a gold handle between the seats and said, "The refrigerator is fully stocked with drinks and snacks if you'd like. Mr. McCoy filled it with items he thought you and Miss Angela would like."

"Thanks Frank," Mike said as he slipped into the rear seat of the limousine. Frank closed the solid door with polished wood paneling. Mike curiously but slowly opened the refrigerator. Inside were cans of Coke and Diet Coke, a couple of bottles of water, some cubed cheese and two apples. On top of the refrigerator sat a sturdy but small wicker basket with an assortment of small bags of chips and pretzels, and a red silky ribbon tied around the handle.

A thick glass pane divided the passenger area from the driver's. Mike could see the back of

Frank's head but couldn't hear him through the window. He felt somewhat secluded and a little silly sitting alone in the spacious limo, especially as there was room for at least nine other passengers. He took note of the flat screen TV, the DVD player, and the crystal and polished wood bar. Looking down at the recently oiled shiny hardwood floor, he chuckled. He couldn't believe the grandeur and even less so, that one person could afford such a vehicle.

They drove to Angela's and parked on the street. "We've arrived Master Mike. Please stay seated until I open your door," Frank calmly announced over the intercom.

The chauffer's voice sounded just like the pilot's when he had flown to California with his parents when he was seven. His dad cupped his hand over his mouth and mimicked everything the Captain said, making his son laugh until his sides hurt.

His most frequent memories were of his dad being silly and his mother laughing at her husband's foolishness. Sometimes, she scolded her husband for his behavior. Other times, heated discussions followed. It didn't matter who was right, each playfully claim to be the victor.

Frank opened the door and stepped aside. As he got out, Mike realized he could get used to this lifestyle. He smiled at his chauffer as he stood up and straightened his shirt.

"You look impeccable sir," Frank offered. "Miss Angela is a very lucky girl indeed."

"Thanks Frank. Truth is I'm the lucky one." Mike smiled with flushed cheeks.

He walked up to the front door and rang the bell. He'd made this walk hundreds of times but had never felt this tense. Mrs. Davis opened the door and greeted him with a huge, friendly smile.

"Hi Mike, come on in. Angela's almost ready. I see you've met our generous new friend, Mr. McCoy. I mean Walter."

"Yes, ma'am. We're using his limo tonight." Mike felt self-conscious as he spoke. He still hadn't come to terms with dating his best friend's little sister. Even so, Mrs. Davis looked no different than when he came to get David to skateboard.

"Walter's an angel. I can't believe how generous he is. He offered to pay for David and Angela's college tuition." She became teary-eyed as she continued, "Can you believe it? He said he was making the same proposition to you and Cedric." Until now, Mrs. Davis had worried whether she could afford to send her kids to college, much less one of their choice.

"Yes, he made us the same offer," Mike responded. "I can't believe it either."

Mrs. Davis laughed and patted Mike's cheek with the palm of her hand. "Such a good boy. Oh, here's Angela!" Mrs. Davis proudly announced as her daughter skip-walked into the room. "Make sure she's home before midnight Mike, just like Cinderella. Got it?"

Captivated by his date's beauty, Mike responded absentmindedly, "Will do, Mrs. Davis."

His eyes had popped wide open when Angela entered. He had never seen her dressed up like this. She looked beautiful in her well-ironed, new jeans and silky, light pink blouse. The clingy fabric highlighted her curvy figure and the heavier than usual makeup emphasized her natural beauty. Her deep brown eyes sparkled behind long, curly lashes and her pouty lips appeared fuller under the soft pink lip gloss. Her large smile showed off her perfect white teeth as she happily greeted him with a "Hi Mike!" His heart missed a beat.

Angela was shocked when she saw the limo out front. Mike grinned broadly, "Walter's surprise. I hope you don't mind. I thought it would be fun."

"No, this is fabulous!" Angela grabbed Mike's arm and hugged it. "There's a good movie at Cielo Vista Mall. It's about some high school kids who accidentally kill a teacher and then have an after school romance."

"Wow. Sounds interesting," Mike mocked a yawn.

"Well that's the best movie. The only other good movie is about a boy and his leopard seal. I really don't want to see that."

Frank got out and opened the door, bowing to Angela as she stepped in and winking at Mike as he entered. As Frank sat down, he cued the intercom and asked, "Where to first, sir?"

"Could you take us to the movie theater at Cielo Vista Mall, please?"

"Of course sir, my pleasure."

The limousine pulled away from the curb as David came around the corner of the block. Mike unrolled the window and waved at him as they passed. His friend returned his wave with two thumbs up and a big smile.

"Did David tell you about last night?"

"Oh my God, Mike! I can't believe some of the things you guys went through."

"What did your mom say?"

"David didn't tell me in front of her. In fact, he asked me to keep it secret."

"Good. The last thing I want is your mom angry at me. The whole thing was my fault. When we crossed the bridge back, I got silly. If it wasn't for that, we wouldn't have missed the party or the buses."

"Think of it this way Mike, if it wasn't for you, no one would have been there to help Mr. McCoy and the other victim. It's weird. It doesn't sound like something you'd do but because of your prank, you had the chance to save lives. I seriously doubt my Mom would get mad at you, but don't worry, my lips are sealed."

"Thanks, I just don't want to rock the boat," Mike had let out another nautical cliché before he could stop himself. He continued, "Your mom's cool. It's bad enough I'm dating you."

"What do you mean bad enough?"

"Well, you know, your mom might not like me taking you out."

"Hardly Mike. It was my mother who suggested I ask you out. She's known how I feel about you for a long time. Mom likes the idea of us dating. You're smart, good-looking - we know where you live..."

Mike laughed, "See? That's what I'm worried about!"

"I'm just teasing. You're like family Mike. No matter what happens, you'll always be family to us."

Mike smiled and nodded. Angela kissed her fingertips and touched Mike's cheek. He blushed, but less than before.

"You make me feel embarrassed. I've never had a girlfriend before," Mike whispered to her.

Angela smiled coyly and gently tickled Mike's ribs. Mike grabbed both of her shoulders, but instead of pushing her away, he pulled her in tight and gave her a big hug.

The limousine came to a stop and Frank opened the door. "We're here, Master Mike. Will you need my service for anything else?"

"No thanks. The movie ends at eight thirty. We'll be out here by eight thirty-five."

"Very well sir. Enjoy your movie."

The theater was dark when they entered and the previews had already started. In typical fashion, Mike headed to the seats in the back of the theater. Angela tugged at Mike's shirtsleeve.

"You're not trying to get me alone in the back seats are you?" Angela whispered in his ear.

Mike immediately turned red and stammered, "No. I always sit in the back."

Angela couldn't see Mike blush in the darkness. She leaned in close and whispered, "Let's find somewhere alone."

Mike smiled. His date shivered as she sat down. He put his arm around her to keep her warm. Angela moved in close, resting her head on his shoulder. The scent of her perfume tickled his nose. Mike was nervous and didn't know what to do. Every scary scene would cause Angela to grab his shirt, sometimes burying her head deep in his chest. Mike found it too distracting and tried hard to focus on the movie. However, when it was over, he couldn't remember much of what he'd seen, but he could vividly recall everything about Angela, especially her soft, honeydew scented hair.

Back at the limo, Mike requested the chauffer take them to dinner. Frank politely nodded, knowing Mike's wishes in advance. Instead of driving in the direction of the surrounding restaurants, he drove homeward.

"I think he's taking us the wrong way. Is he taking us home?" It was obvious to Mike she didn't want the date to end, but he didn't want to spoil Walter's surprise. Her concern would only make it that much sweeter.

"No, he's going in the right direction." Mike smiled and winked at Angela.

"You're not taking me to Chico's Tacos are you?" Angela asked with a giggle. "Or to your house?"

"Of course not. It's a surprise," Mike tried to suppress his amusement. He wanted to blurt out the evening's plans but kept quiet instead.

Frank pulled up to Angela's house and parked. She shot Mike a quizzical look as David and Cedric appeared in the doorway. Frank got out and opened the door. The boys laughed as they piled into the limousine.

"Hi Angie!" Cedric said as he sat facing the couple. "Sure was nice of Mike to invite us!"

"I didn't expect you two tonight! I thought this was a date." She glared at Mike, puzzled and perturbed.

"I invited them. You'll see why Angela."

Frank headed west on Interstate 10. He took the downtown exit and headed south past the Plaza. Everyone was talking, laughing and having a good time. Everyone - except Angela. She stared out the window, in her own world of thought, wishing she were alone with Mike but curious to see the evening unfold.

She had never been to a restaurant in this part of town. In fact, she wasn't even sure if there were any restaurants.

The limo went straight through town and into the southern section which was packed densely with small stores and currency changing stands. "Casa de Cambio," "Telas de Rio Bravo," "Liberty Army Supply." Beyond the stores lay the bridge to Mexico. Angela was sure the limo would turn on one of the side streets, instead it kept going straight for the border.

"Mike, tell me where we're going," Angela demanded sternly, her worries showing.

"We're going to eat a delicacy. Last night we had what is possibly the world's best food. I want you to try it. Tonight is not an ordinary night - it's the first after a life-changing event. I wanted us all to be a part of it."

"I refuse to eat monkey brains or cow tongue," Angela wrinkled her nose as she made her proclamation.

"How about Dog Tacos?" Cedric laughed.

Mike shot his friend a hardened stare. "Relax Angela. You're going to love this place! We're almost there."

The limousine made its way across the bridge. The usual weekend partiers were out on a Saturday evening. Hundreds of tourists either on foot or in cars eagerly moved along. Interspersed were a few laborers and maids returning home after a long day of work in El Paso. Hovering in the area were the same vendors from the evening before and in full force as usual.

Angela was glued to the window, completely oblivious to the excited discussions of the prior night's events involving the three teenagers sharing her date. She was scared and mesmerized by the flurry of night activity and strange people on the other side of the glass. She had always heard young girls shouldn't be out in Juarez at night because they get kidnapped and sold into the sex slave trade. She also knew that hundreds of young girls had been brutally murdered. A serial killer or killers had been kidnapping, raping, mutilating, and killing young girls since 1993. These frightening accounts raced through her mind and expanded in her imagination.

A thousand thoughts away Cedric laughed at how Uncle Ralph saved them from the Homeless Gang with a military smoke bomb and an empty M-16. David added, "And then you called him Uncle Rambo!" Cedric's cleverness after their face-off with the infamous Homeless Gang had not only amused the friends the prior evening, but had provided a sense of relief, security and familiarity.

Undeniably, Uncle Ralph was quite a character. Mike laughed along as he looked out the window at the discothèques now in full view. Long, endless lines of people spilled out onto the street, waiting impatiently. Some stood on their tiptoes with heads outstretched trying to get a good look. All eagerly anticipated the drinking and dancing that awaited them inside. Even though it was less than two miles from her house, Angela had never been to Juarez. Seeing the disco patrons both excited and panicked her at once. There were so many young, wildly dressed people. She had never seen anything like it.

She couldn't make out the colors of the buildings lighted by the dim streetlights. Red became gray; yellow, white; blue, black. Every disco and storefront on the main strip glowed in massive quantities of reds, blues, yellows, greens and more colors than she'd ever seen in neon. Juarez was surreal, scary, seductive.

The Town Car slowed and made a right turn on a narrow, dark street. Dog Tacos quietly sat, tucked in the middle of the block - its doors closed, void of any customers.

"Why are we stopping here?" Angela asked anxiously. "I'm seriously worried. What's really up?" The more she spoke, the more apprehensive she became.

Ignoring Angela's concerns Mike asked, "Hey Frank, how'd Walter do this? I mean they've shut down for us, this is incredible."

"Mr. McCoy is an appreciative man and he's good friends with the owner. He's really gone out for you. You've brought a new enthusiasm into his life. You truly saved him, in more ways than you can know…" Frank's voice drifted off.

Mike had heard it straight from Walter this afternoon and had been reflecting on this destined connection. Life was more than a thousand breaths, brainwaves, and a pumping heart.

"OK now, sirs and lady," Frank broke the silence. "Your feast awaits you."

"Feast?" Mike queried.

"You'll see Master Mike. Everything's been taken care of."

"Master Mike!" Cedric teased. "Boy you've sure come a long way since last night - gotten all uppity on us."

"Please Master Cedric," Frank panned. "I was trained in England. I truly hope you don't mind."

Cedric blushed. "I don't mind Frank, but it will take some getting used to. Never been called Master anything before."

Mike and Angela reached the door first. They pushed it and stepped inside. The ledge along the wall that during regular hours served as a bar for those who chose to stay and eat was laid out with bright and colorful little bowls of salsas of every imaginable type. In the center of the small room was a card table with a bright blue tablecloth and brightly colored ceramic plates already filled with tacos. On the floor next to the table was a large silver tub of ice with a variety of cold sodas including pineapple, tangerine, and apple. Near the door on a table with a bright red and yellow striped serape sat a large glass container filled with five gallons of horchata, the drink that had mercifully saved Mike from overdosing the night before.

"Wow," Angela said. "This place is so tiny, colorful, pretty - it feels like we're in a different, faraway country."

Mike laughed. "The tacos are incredible. Beware of the salsa. It'll sneak up on you. Start with just a little and add more if you can stand it."

David and Cedric marveled at the spread set out just for them. David hurriedly picked up one of the tiny tacos and devoured it. Like a world class chef judging the finest cuisine, he closed his eyes to savor the flavor and sighed like he was in heaven.

"Can you believe this? I don't know where to start. Should I have a taco, or maybe a taco? What should I have first? I think I'll have a taco," Cedric joked.

Picking up a second taco, David said, "Doesn't matter where you start, it's where you end up that counts. I'm trying for a dozen or more tonight. Crown me the Taco King right now!"

"I'm pretty sure I can eat two dozen." Cedric countered.

"You're on, Taco Boy," David wagered.

Mike and Angela served their plates, carefully and minimally spooning salsa.

As they set their dishes down, Mike pulled her chair out. She grabbed his warm hand and squeezed it, then edged closer, kissing his cheek lightly. Not waiting for him to reciprocate, she hugged him tightly and whispered, "Thanks, Mikey. This is the best surprise."

Mike's mind raced with thoughts of kissing her, and he would have had David not been in the same room. Instead, eyeing the drinks, he matter-of-factly offered, "You want a glass of horchata or a soda?"

"Horchata?"

"It's watery sweet rice milk with cinnamon. It's really good. Plus, it'll help cool down the salsa burn. I can vouch for that first-hand."

"OK, horchata sounds good."

Mike got their drinks and sat down. As soon as he picked up his taco, she caught his hand and pulled the treat in her direction, promptly biting it. The taco was so small that this time he could clearly see the damage.

"Gosh, this is so delicious," Angela sighed, setting down her glass. "I would've never guessed everything here would be so good."

"Cedric calls this place Dog Tacos because of the three German Shepherds living above, but its real name is El Taquito Mexicano. They have the best tacos I've ever had."

"No way! Better than Chico's?" Angela knew how devoted Mike was to his rolled tacos and found this hard to believe.

"I never thought I'd find a place I like as much as Chico's, but Dog Tacos rules. It's my new favorite!" Mike proclaimed but then as if to relieve himself of any guilt, he pounded his chest twice and threw a gang sign that looked like a C, adding, "Chico's for life!"

"So what do you think about Mr. McCoy?" Angela asked. "Mom said he offered to pay for our college - wherever we want to go. Can you believe that? It's . . . It's insane! Yesterday morning none of us had ever heard of him. Tonight. . ."

"I'm still pretty freaked out. If it weren't for the limo outside, I still wouldn't believe it. Walter's an amazing guy."

"I'm so glad we finally went out," Angela whispered. "Thanks for such a wonderful evening." She kissed his right cheek as she spoke, her warm breath exciting him. "My hero," she whispered into his ear, sending chills down his spine.

"You should thank Walter. He's the one who made this happen," Mike said.

"No Mike," Angela said somewhat curtly. "If we only took a walk around the block tonight, I would've been perfectly happy. Yes, Walter's a nice man and he did nice things for us tonight, but being with you is what makes me happiest. That's all I need." Angela sighed and shook her head as she spoke. "You'll understand someday. All I want is to be with you, it doesn't matter what we do. It's the time we spend together that counts."

"What could be better than this?" Mike asked loudly, not expecting an answer. "I've got a date who's both beautiful and smart, two great friends and all the Dog Tacos I can eat."

Mike toasted by raising his glass of horchata into the air. Cedric and David immediately raised their tacos in toast. Angela simply giggled at the sight.

Suddenly, the front door swung open and Walter walked in. An older Mexican man with a large silver belt buckle and cowboy boots followed, greeting the cooks as he entered. Together, they sauntered toward the patrons.

"Hi boys, Angela," Walter nodded, tipping the cowboy hat he was wearing. "I've someone here I'd like you to meet. Mike, David, Cedric, Angela allow me to introduce my good friend Señor Lozano, taco restaurateur."

Señor Lozano waved everyone to remain seated and spoke in accented English. "Welcome to my estableeshment. I am honored to provide service to jou. We have been here for tirty tree years."

Mike saluted their host. "My compliments to the chefs," he announced, lifting a taco in their direction. The small lady smiled proudly before returning to her task.

"I have jus one question, por favor," Señor Lozano leaned closer and spoke in a deep, hushed whisper. "Wheech one of jou calls thees place Dog Tacos?"

Cedric turned bright red - the culprit had been identified. Señor Lozano walked over and put his hand on the embarrassed boy's shoulder.

"I thought so. Jou look like a jokester. Dog Tacos. Ha! I would not allow it." Señor Lozano's teeth clenched slightly as he spoke.

"I was only joking," Cedric replied defensively.

"Those dogs are our pets!"

Cedric laughed somewhat shakily, "There were three German shepherds, right?"

"Jes! Paco, Pancho Villa and Selena. I would never think to cook them! My daughters would keel me, eh?" Señor Lozano nudged Cedric, winking with a wry smile.

"That's a relief!" Cedric exclaimed.

"Well having solved that mystery, we're off to Santa Teresa! It was splendeed meeting jou all."

"We're having dinner at Señor Lozano's new restaurant at the country club," Walter clarified. "You kids enjoy the rest of the night. By the way,

Mrs. Davis has extended your curfew to one o'clock - she wanted me to pass the message."

"Thanks for everything, Walter, Señor Lozano." Mike stood and shook their hands. "You really made our night."

"Don't mention it Mike. It's my honor," Walter beamed. Señor Lozano winked at the group as he turned toward the door. Just as quickly as they had arrived, the gentlemen were gone.

Mike and Angela had eaten their fill, but the friends were still competing. The count was nine, David, and twelve for Cedric. The chefs had prepared six more tacos for each competitor. All bets were on Cedric who continued eating with gusto while David was far less enthusiastic.

Two bites into his tenth taco David groaned, "I'm done. . ."

"Suit yourself," Cedric laughed maniacally. "I win! Suckah!"

Accepting defeat and feeling fifty pounds heavier, David turned to Mike, "Are the ove-lay ird-bays ready to go?"

"Ove-lay ird-bays what?" Cedric questioned.

"Love birds! It's pig Latin for love birds!" David abruptly replied, revealing his annoyance with Cedric's victory. "Let's call it a night, OK?"

The friends all left El Taquito Mexicano and headed toward their limo, each carrying two bags filled with tacos and salsa. Frank opened the car door. Angela ducked in but Mike stopped and handed a bag to Frank, "Take these tacos, please. They're for you and Mr. McCoy."

"And who may I ask is the second bag for, Master Mike?" Frank asked raising his eyebrow in mock curiosity.

"Tacos for our second date tomorrow," Mike whispered.

David and Cedric made kissing sounds and snickered as Mike's face reddened. Ignoring the two bozos, Mike slid into the limo, turning his attention to Angela.

The limousine pulled up to the main street, 16 de Septiembre. The town was still in the throes of its Saturday night crowds. Cars, tourists, disco patrons, taxi drivers, beggars and assorted revelers crowded the four blocks of Mexico that led to the bridge back to the United States.

Frank pulled up to the main street and waited. Waving at a group of men, they went into action. Two of them blocked traffic, while the third directed Frank onto the street. Frank rolled down his window and passed a roll of bills to one of the men.

"Gracias Manuel, eh," Frank said to the man.

"Por nada Francisco, por nada."

Manuel walked over to the sidewalk where his compadres were waiting. They looked at Frank and waved. Frank nodded, yelling, "Gracias Juan, gracias Jorge!"

"Who were those guys?" David asked through the intercom.

"Manuel is my uncle. Juan and Jorge are my cousins but they're more like brothers - we were all raised by my grandmother."

"And they just happened to be in the area when we needed them?"

"Not exactly," he smiled mysteriously.

"Do they live close by?" Cedric interrogated.

"They live in New Mexico, Master Cedric. They operate pistachio and pecan orchards there."

"And they came all the way to stop traffic for us?" David was perplexed.

"They had business in town and offered to help out. Walter's been their silent partner for many years. They've done very well."

"Oh..." the boys finally understood.

The limo slowly made its way across the bridge. Midway, a rogue fire-eater improvised his performance as his vivacious assistants collected donations from passing cars and pedestrians.

Cedric jabbed David in the side, pointing at Mike. "Make sure this one claims the right nationality tonight. Don't need to spend another night in customs."

"Yeah," David added, staring sternly at Mike, "American citizen! OK?"

"I got it. No trouble tonight," Mike guaranteed his friends just as the limo pulled up to the checkpoint.

The burly agent leaned in and scanned the occupants, "Nationalities?"

"American," all declared in unison.

"OK. You can pass," the customs agent officially waved the group through.

"See Mike," David said. "That's how you get back into America. Pretty simple, eh?"

"OK. I got it," Mike responded defensively. "Never again. OK?"

"Sure Mike." Taking note of Mike's irritation, David held back. Instead he turned to Cedric and pulled him into a separate conversation.

"Yes," Angela whispered, edging up to Mike.

"Yes, what?" Mike was dumbfounded as if suddenly awakened, wondering what he'd missed.

"Yes, Mike. I'll go out with you tomorrow! And eat micro-waved Dog Tacos!"

He laughed, "What makes you think I'm asking?"

"I heard you tell Frank, silly!"

"Shhh," Mike hushed Angela, noticing Cedric and David had fallen asleep. "They're probably pretty tired after all that's happened."

Angela slid even closer to Mike and gently laid her head on his shoulder, her silky hair covering his arm and her soft breath caressing his neck. After a while, he leaned over. She was fast asleep. He tenderly kissed her head and drifted into thought.

He wondered what his parents would think about his adventures. Would his dad have saved the day like Uncle Ralph? Would he have even been able to go skating downtown?

He was aware his life and that of his friends had just taken a big turn. Suddenly, the world was open to them. Wherever they would go in life, he hoped they would always remain close.

Moments later, Frank looked in the rearview mirror. He saw four teenagers whose lives were about to change dramatically. Four teenagers who would never be the same thanks to heroic deeds and acts of generosity. Four teenagers sleeping in the back of a limo on the biggest night of their lives.

Frank chuckled to himself and looked over at the full bag of tacos on the passenger seat, "I like these kids."

Dog Tacos

Orphaned at nine, seventeen year old Mike is absorbed with skateboarding and dreams of someday going to college. His obsessions are fueled by his festering anger and resentment over his parents' tragic and untimely deaths, and a desire to be the first college graduate in the family.

Although he lives in poverty with his kindhearted grandmother and alcoholic uncle, Mike feels lucky. His doting grandmother works hard to give him a good life. His psychologically tormented uncle fights post-war demons but tries to be there for his nephew. His best friend David, whose sister Angela has a crush on Mike, has been like a brother. Mike's loyalty to his sport, family and friends is unbreakable.

It's Friday and Mike wakes up brutalized from a boardslide gone awry the night before. Despite his cuts, bruises and sore muscles, Mike can't wait to skateboard tonight. He, David and Cedric have planned to skate in the forbidden zone downtown and go to a party afterwards. Cedric has an added surprise for his buddies - dinner across the border in Mexico at a suspicious looking little hole in the wall he calls Dog Tacos.

Before the night is over, the friends will come face-to-face with the most notorious gang in town, be detained and interrogated at the U.S. border and be hailed as heroes on the local news. Mike's heart and loyalty will also be tested. This night will challenge the friends like no other. The unexpected rewards far outweigh the night's events.